W ELCOME TO THIS COLLECTION
of stories about Samantha Parkington, an
orphan being raised by her wealthy Victorian
grandmother as America begins a brand-new
century. Samantha's own world is filled with
frills and finery, but she sees that times are not
good for everybody. Samantha dares to make a
difference, befriending people and going places
and saying things a "proper young lady" isn't
supposed to. Because of girls like Samantha,
America's ideas about what women and girls
can and cannot do are about to change.

Together in this special edition, Samantha's
stories will capture girls' imaginations for years
to come. Step inside Samantha's world of newfangled notions and fantastic inventions, and be
inspired all over again.

Samantha
STORY
COLLECTION

By SUSAN S. ADLER,
MAXINE ROSE SCHUR,
AND VALERIE TRIPP

ILLUSTRATIONS BY
DAN ANDREASEN

★ AmericanGirl®

Published by American Girl Publishing, Inc.
Copyright © 2001, 2008 by American Girl, LLC

Questions or comments? Call 1-800-845-0005, visit our Web site
at **americangirl.com**, or write to Customer Service, American Girl,
8400 Fairway Place, Middleton, WI 53562-0497.

Printed in China
08 09 10 11 12 13 14 LEO 10 9 8 7 6 5 4 3 2 1

All American Girl marks, Samantha®, Samantha Parkington®,
Nellie™, and Nellie O'Malley™ are trademarks of American Girl, LLC.

PICTURE CREDITS
The following individuals and organizations have generously
given permission to reprint images contained in "Looking Back":
p. 361—Brown Brothers; pp. 362–363—Culver Pictures; Brown Brothers;
Brown Brothers; Wisconsin Historical Society; The Bettmann Archive;
pp. 364–365—Mrs. Lora Timm; C.J. Hibbard, Minnesota Historical
Society; Wisconsin Historical Society; Jane Addams Memorial Collection,
Special Collections, The University Library, University of Illinois at Chicago;
Jane Addams Memorial Collection, Special Collections, The University
Library, University of Illinois at Chicago; Wisconsin Historical Society;
pp. 366–367—Wisconsin Historical Society; Cincinnati Art Museum,
Purchase; gift of Mrs. J. Louis Ransohoff, by exchange; Culver Pictures;
Reprinted with permission of Butterick Company, Inc.,
161 Avenue of the Americas, New York, NY 10013.

Vignette Illustrations by Jana Fothergill, Renée Graef,
Eileen Potts Dawson, and Luann Roberts

Cataloging-in-Publication Data available from the Library of Congress.

TABLE OF CONTENTS

SAMANTHA'S FAMILY AND FRIENDS

SAMANTHA'S FAMILY

GRANDMARY
Samantha's grandmother, who wants her to be a young lady

NELLIE
The girl who lives—and works— next door

SAMANTHA
A nine-year-old orphan who lives with her wealthy grandmother

UNCLE GARD
Samantha's favorite uncle, who calls her "Sam"

CORNELIA
An old-fashioned beauty who has newfangled ideas

HAWKINS
*Grandmary's butler
and driver, who is
Samantha's friend*

MRS. HAWKINS
*The cook, who
always has a treat
for Samantha*

ELSA
*The maid, who
is usually grumpy*

JESSIE
*Grandmary's
seamstress, who
"patches Samantha up"*

EDDIE
*Samantha's
neighbor, who loves
to tease*

IDA DEAN
*Samantha's friend,
who is planning
the best Christmas
party ever*

AGNES & AGATHA
*Samantha's newest
friends, who are
Cornelia's sisters*

ADMIRAL
ARCHIBALD BEEMIS
*A jolly Englishman
who visits Grandmary
every summer*

TO MY PARENTS,
WHO MADE CHILDHOOD
BEAUTIFUL

MEET

Samantha

BY SUSAN S. ADLER

JESSIE

"Samantha!"

The voice broke through the summer afternoon like a crack. The leaves of the quiet old oak tree suddenly rustled and dropped a squirming bundle of arms and legs. Samantha Parkington tumbled out of the tree.

"Samantha, you're really dumb," the voice continued. It was coming from a hole in the hedge that separated Samantha's house from Eddie Ryland's. "You're so dumb, you don't even know how to climb a tree."

Samantha glanced at her scraped and bleeding knee and looked pained—not because of the knee, but because the voice was at it again. She glared at

1

its owner with a look that could have frozen water in July. "Go away, Eddie."

But Eddie's round, sticky face didn't go away. "You're so dumb, you probably think three times four is twelve," he said.

"Eddie." Samantha looked disgusted. "Three times four *is* twelve."

"Well, anyway, you're so dumb—"

That was enough for Samantha. "Eddie," she said, "if you don't get out of here right now, I will take your entire beetle collection from behind the shed, and I'll put it in the offering plate at church on Sunday." She paused to be sure he was listening. "And I'll tell your mother *you* did it."

Eddie's eyes grew wide. He pulled his mouth into a frog face and left to find a safer hiding place for his beetle collection.

Samantha examined her knee. The bleeding had stopped, but her stocking was badly torn. She could picture how Grandmary would look when she saw it. Grandmary's eyes had a soft, warm light when they looked at Samantha, but her face could be very stern when she talked about

2

growing up. "Discipline," Grandmary always said, "is what turns girls into ladies."

Samantha tugged at the hole in her stocking, but she couldn't hide it. The taffeta bow that had held her dark brown hair drooped over her forehead. Yes, this was a job for Jessie.

Samantha hurried up the walk and climbed the porch steps two at a time. At the front door, she slowed down. If there was any noise at the front door, Elsa might come. Elsa was the new maid. She was always grumpy, and Samantha didn't want to listen to a lecture now.

Luckily, the door was quiet. No one saw Samantha run all the way to the third floor. There, at the end of the hall, was the sewing room. And in the corner sat Jessie. Yards and yards of soft pink material tumbled around her, and the sewing machine clicked quietly as her feet pressed the treadle back and forth. She hummed to its rhythm as her fine hands guided the cloth past the flashing needle.

Jessie made clothes for the household. She was working on a new dress for Grandmary, but she stopped as Samantha came through the door.

"Oh, Miss Samantha, just look at you," Jessie said. As she stood and turned, Jessie's large floating apron swirled over the baskets of thread and laces that rested on the floor. "What have you been up to? No, don't tell me. I don't want to know. Here you are, nine years old, almost a lady, and still getting into mischief like a ragamuffin. What will your Grandmary say?"

Samantha folded her hands and looked at the floor until Jessie was quiet. The mild scolding was a small price to pay for the help she knew Jessie would give her. Already Jessie had brushed the

"Here you are, nine years old, almost a lady, and still getting into mischief like a ragamuffin," said Jessie.

grass and dust from her hair. Now she checked
Samantha's dress for tears and stains. She spotted
the torn stocking.

"Take off those shoes and stockings right now.
Does your knee hurt?" asked Jessie.

"No, Jessie, it's all right. I'd just rather not have
to explain to Grandmary," said Samantha.

Jessie smiled and reached for her sewing basket.
Samantha found a small clean rag and wet it from
the water pitcher. She sponged her injured knee
while Jessie sat down to repair the damaged
stocking.

As Samantha looked around the
room, she noticed a piece of jelly
biscuit on the floor. She must have
dropped it the day before. Three ants
had found it. She was about to tell Jessie when she
noticed two more ants on their way. It would be
fun to see how many would come.

Samantha sighed loudly. "It must be awfully
boring to be grown up," she said.

Jessie laughed softly. "Well, that depends. It
depends a lot on the person. Now you, Miss
Samantha, I don't think you'll have to be worried

about being bored, even when you're grown up."

There were seven ants on the jelly biscuit now.

"I'll bet Cornelia isn't bored," said Samantha.

Jessie laughed again. "No, I don't imagine Miss Cornelia is very often bored," she said. Cornelia was a friend of Samantha's favorite uncle. She was pretty and dark haired, and she laughed easily. Anyone could see that she liked Uncle Gard a lot. But Samantha didn't think Cornelia was right for Uncle Gard. She thought someone like Alice Roosevelt, the President's daughter, would be better. Alice Roosevelt did the most exciting things, and the newspapers were always talking about her.

"Is Uncle Gard going to marry Cornelia?" asked Samantha.

Alice Roosevelt

"That's none of our business," Jessie said firmly. "And children shouldn't ask such questions."

Samantha grumbled softly. "A minute ago I was almost a lady. Now I'm a child again."

Twelve ants were on the biscuit, and three were on the way.

"Uncle Gard is a spy, you know," Samantha said.

"Miss Samantha!" Jessie's head shot up in surprise. "Where do you get such foolish ideas?"

"Well, he *should* be a spy," Samantha went on. "He's so handsome and brave, everyone would just fall in love with him. He could get their secrets, and they'd be so in love with him, they wouldn't even care."

"I think you'd better keep such ideas to yourself," Jessie said as she looked closely at the hole she was mending. "You've made quite enough trouble for one day."

There were nineteen ants around the jelly biscuit.

"Jessie, did you know my mother and father?" Samantha asked.

Jessie spoke gently. "You know I didn't, child. That accident in the boat happened when you were just five. You know I didn't come to work for your grandmother till you were seven."

Samantha had known that. Asking had really been wishing. She touched the locket pinned to her

8

dress. Inside the small gold heart was a picture of her mother and father. She would have loved to hear Jessie talk about them. When Jessie told stories, she made everything sound like magic. Jessie would have made Samantha's parents seem like a prince and princess.

"Tell me about New Orleans, Jessie. Please?"

Jessie picked up a piece of silk for the sleeve of Grandmary's new dress. Her musical voice began to tell about a place where flowers bloomed in winter, a place where there were huge white mansions and balconies made of iron that looked like lace. She told about spicy shrimp and about music and dancing in the streets. And the best part was, every-thing Jessie said was true. She didn't have to make up stories about faraway places. Her husband, Lincoln, was a porter on the train that ran to New Orleans. Lincoln brought home wonderful tales of the places he'd seen and the people he'd met. And he never forgot Samantha. She had a scrapbook almost full of colorful postcards that he sent her from all of his trips. Sometimes he brought her pralines from New Orleans—brown sugary candy crowded with sweet pecans. Jessie and Lincoln made Samantha's world wide and wonderful. An hour passed easily with Jessie's soft voice carrying Samantha to dreamlike places.

A NEW GIRL

At four o'clock, Samantha stood
outside the parlor doors, looking like
new. It was time for her hour with
Grandmary. Samantha's hair was combed, her
ribbon was perfect, her skirt hung straight, and her
stockings were repaired. She knocked softly on the
door, then slipped through and made a quick curtsy
to her grandmother.

Samantha thought Grandmary looked like
a queen, especially during their sewing hour.
Grandmary sat up very straight. Her velvet chair
looked like a throne with her silk gown flowing
around it. Her white hair seemed made for a crown,
with never a strand out of place.

Samantha always *tried* to be a young lady, but it was a lot easier to remember how when Grandmary was watching. Samantha noticed that everyone behaved more like a lady when Grandmary was around.

"Good afternoon, Samantha," said Grandmary.

"Good afternoon, Grandmary." Samantha squirmed ever so slightly. She didn't know how, but Grandmary always seemed to know when she had been into mischief. But today Grandmary didn't ask questions. Instead, she smiled.

"Come sit down, my dear," Grandmary said.

She handed a small basket to Samantha. "You must try to work a little harder on your sampler. It's not going very quickly."

"Yes, Grandmary." Samantha took her seat on a chair next to her grandmother. She picked up her sampler and sighed a little. When it was finished, the sampler would read "ACTIONS SPEAK LOUDER THAN WORDS." Grandmary had explained this saying. She said it meant that how people act is more important than what they say. Samantha tried to imagine the words sewn in pink silk thread. Around them would be flowers and fruits made of complicated stitches that would show off her sewing skills. But the skills were slow in coming. So far the sampler read "ACTIONS SP."

Samantha stuck her tongue between her lips as she concentrated on a hard stitch. She glanced sideways to see if her grandmother looked in a good mood.

"Grandmary," Samantha began.

"Yes, dear?"

"Did you see the doll in Schofield's shop?" Samantha asked.

"Yes, dear, I did," answered Grandmary.

"Isn't she beautiful?" sighed Samantha.

"It's quite a nice doll," Grandmary said.

"Do you think I might have her?"

"Samantha, that is an expensive doll," said Grandmary. "It costs six dollars. If you are going to grow up to be a responsible young lady, you must understand the value of a dollar."

"I could earn the money to buy her, Grandmary. I could make boomerangs and sell them. *The Boys' Handy Book* shows just how to do it. I could—"

"Samantha!" Grandmary was shocked. "A *lady* does not earn money."

Samantha had known there wasn't much hope, but she added very quietly, "Cornelia says a woman should be able to earn money. She says women shouldn't have to depend on men for everything. She says—"

"Cornelia has a great many newfangled

14

notions," announced Grandmary. "She should keep them to herself."

Samantha turned back to her work with a sigh. "I would have called the doll Lydia," she said softly. "She looks like my mother."

Grandmary was startled. Then her eyes softened. A moment later she said, "There are other ways, my dear, to reach your goals."

Samantha looked up hopefully. Grandmary continued, "If you do well at your tasks, you might earn the doll. If you practice your piano daily—"

"Oh, Grandmary, I will." Samantha was delighted. "I'll practice an hour every day. I'll make my sampler beautiful. I'll help Mrs. Hawkins. I won't get my dress muddy. I—" She was about to say she wouldn't tease Eddie Ryland, but she knew there were some promises she just couldn't keep. "Oh, Grandmary, thank you!" Samantha threw her arms around her grandmother's neck.

"There, there, my dear. We shall see," said Grandmary with a slight note of caution in her voice. "We shall see how you do."

Samantha worked hard on her sampler for half an hour. Then, from down the street, she heard a low rumble. Soon there were great pops and bangs. As the noise grew louder, angry voices and the frightened whinnies of horses joined it. Samantha jumped up from her seat and ran to the window.

"Oh, Grandmary, it's Uncle Gard. It's Uncle Gard and Cornelia!" Samantha called.

Grandmary raised her eyes to the ceiling. "He's brought that dreadful automobile again. Whatever shall I tell the neighbors!"

Samantha could hardly contain her excitement as the shiny black car jerked and sputtered to a stop in front of the house. Two people climbed out. They wore long coats that covered them from head to toe. Cornelia wore a hat tied down with a scarf, and Uncle Gard wore large goggles that made him look like an overgrown fly. They came up the walk laughing and beating the dust from their hats and coats.

The bell rang. A minute later, Hawkins appeared at the parlor door looking dignified. It seemed to Samantha that the more confusion there was, the more dignified Hawkins became. "Mister Gardner and Miss Cornelia, Madam," he said.

"Very well, Hawkins. Show them in. And tell Elsa to bring tea," said Grandmary.

"Oh, Grandmary, it's Uncle Gard.
It's Uncle Gard and Cornelia!" Samantha called.

The couple burst into the room, bringing laughter and the smell of summer with them. "How are you, Mother? You look wonderful," said Uncle Gard. He gave Grandmary a big hug, and she couldn't help smiling.

"Good afternoon, Gardner. Good afternoon, Cornelia," said Grandmary. "I am fine, thank you, Gardner. But I was a good deal better before you shattered the peace of the entire neighborhood with that horrible machine of yours. Why must you bring it here?"

Uncle Gard's eyes were laughing. "Now, Mother, this is 1904. You've got to keep up with the times. Besides," he winked at Samantha, "how can I teach Sam to drive if I don't bring the automobile?"

"Oh, Uncle Gard, will you really? Will you?" Samantha was popping with excitement.

"Sure I will. Come on. I'll take you for a ride right now."

"Indeed, you won't," said Grandmary. "What can you be thinking of? Why, her clothes would be ruined!"

Samantha's face fell.

Cornelia looked at her quickly and said, "It's all right. She can wear my duster. It's a little too big, but we'll make it fit, won't we, Samantha?"

duster

As they walked into the hall to fix the coat, Samantha gave Cornelia a grateful smile. Minutes later, she headed down the walk, trailing the hem of the long coat behind her.

Eddie Ryland had been sitting in the car, but he scampered down as Samantha and her uncle approached.

Uncle Gard lifted Samantha up to the seat. "Hold tight, Sam, while I crank it up," he said.

"You sure look dumb, Samantha," Eddie teased. He never stopped.

Samantha wasn't listening. She held tight as Uncle Gard cranked and the car began to lurch.

"Anyway, I know something you don't know," Eddie said loudly so that Samantha could hear him as the car rumbled.

Uncle Gard jumped into the seat next to Samantha and took hold of the steering wheel. The car began to bounce and sway into the middle of the road.

19

"A girl's coming to live at our house. She's nine, just like you," Eddie hollered over the noise.

"You're lying, Eddie Ryland!" Samantha yelled and choked on the dust.

"I am not! Her name's Nellie!"

Samantha didn't even try to answer. She was holding on for dear life as that most modern of inventions, the automobile, bucked and rumbled its way toward town.

Back at the front door, Grandmary shook her head. Just as she turned back to the parlor to join Cornelia for a cup of tea, she saw Jessie scurrying from the kitchen. There was something in her hand.

"Jessie, what's the matter?" asked Grandmary.

As Jessie hurried up the stairs, she called over her shoulder, "It's pepper for the sewing room, ma'am. There are ants up there. Hundreds and hundreds of ants!"

THE TUNNEL

Several days later, Samantha bounded into her backyard holding a gingerbread cookie. She had just finished practicing the piano. She practiced piano every day now, for one whole hour. That hour certainly did seem long. She couldn't wait to get outside when it was over.

Samantha took a deep breath of summer air and a couple of long leaps. She stopped beside the tunnel.

The tunnel was a hole worn in the lilac hedge between her house and the Rylands', but Samantha had always called it "the tunnel." Through it now, she could see a girl. The girl was busy hanging laundry in the Rylands' yard. Could Eddie possibly have been telling the truth? Had this girl really come to live there? Samantha ducked through the tunnel and came closer.

"Are you Nellie?" she asked brightly.

The girl looked surprised and very timid. "Yes, miss," she answered without stopping her work. Eddie had said Nellie was nine, but this girl seemed smaller than Samantha.

"Are you visiting the Rylands?" asked Samantha.

This time Nellie looked amused. "Oh, no, miss. I'm working here," she said.

Samantha was surprised. Eddie hadn't said a girl was coming to *work*. But it didn't matter. Samantha thought it would be wonderful to have a friend right next door. She remembered the cookie in her hand. "Would you like some gingerbread?" she asked. "It's just baked."

Nellie looked at the Rylands' house. "Oh, no, miss. I can't."

"Won't they let you?" asked Samantha.

"No, I don't think so, miss. I've got my job to do," Nellie answered.

"My name's Samantha. You don't have to call

me 'miss.'" Samantha put her cookie and napkin down on a stone and reached for a piece of wet laundry. "I'll help you, Nellie. Then we can play."

"Oh, no, you shouldn't," Nellie said. She was embarrassed, but there was nothing she could do to stop her new friend. So instead, she hurried to finish the job before anyone could see Samantha working.

When the last of the laundry was hung, Samantha grabbed Nellie's hand and pulled her toward the tunnel. "We can eat in here. Nobody will see us," Samantha said. The girls just fit into the hole in the hedge, and Nellie couldn't say no to the spicy smell of gingerbread.

"Why are you working here?" Samantha asked between bites.

Nellie didn't look at Samantha when she answered. "My father works in a factory in the city, and my mother does washing. But there's three of us children, you see, and it's not enough." She added quietly, "There wasn't enough food. And there wasn't enough coal."

Samantha's eyes were wide with disbelief. She

was good at imagining castles and jungles and sailing ships, but she had never imagined hunger and cold. "You mean your parents sent you away? But that's awful!"

"Oh, no. It's better here. It really is," said Nellie. "The Rylands pay my family a dollar a week for the work I do. That's not as much as I earned in the factory, but in the factory I had to work every day but Sunday, until dark. And the air was so hot and dusty, I started coughing a lot. That's why my parents let me come here. The air is good, and I don't have to work so long, and I get good food." With one finger, she collected the last of the cookie crumbs. "Only I don't get to see my family much."

Samantha was shocked into silence, but only for a moment. "When do you go to school?" she asked.

"I've never been to school," Nellie said quietly.

Was it possible? This girl had never gone to school? Samantha's mind raced. "Nellie, I have an idea," she said. "We can meet here every day, and I'll teach you. The Rylands won't miss you for just a little while, and I'll teach you *everything.*"

Nellie's eyes glittered with excitement as the

"There wasn't enough food. And there wasn't enough coal,"
said Nellie.

girls made plans. Then Samantha began talking about everyone she lived with and all the neighbors. By the time she'd told Nellie about Uncle Gard's automobile, they were both giggling.

The girls were interrupted by a familiar voice. "I see you, Samantha! I see you, Nellie! And you're really ugly. You're both so ugly, you'd scare a moose. You're so ugly—"

"Eddie, get out of here," Samantha snapped.

"I'm telling!"

Eddie started toward the house. Nellie looked frightened, but Samantha yelled "Eddie!" in a voice that made him think he'd better wait to hear what she had to say. "Eddie, if you tell anybody anything about us, I will take your new pocketknife and I will stuff it full of taffy."

Eddie stopped. He stared at Samantha. Then he put his hand over his back pocket to protect his knife. He began to back away from the girls. Finally, he ran away.

When he'd gone, Nellie jumped up. "I'd better get back to work," she said.

Samantha followed her out of the tunnel. "All right. But tomorrow we'll make a telephone.

Mrs. Hawkins will give us two tin cans, and I can get a string. We'll string it through the hedge, where Eddie won't see it. Then we can talk whenever we want to. Oh, Nellie, we'll have the most wonderful time!"

C H A P T E R

F O U R

GONE!

By next Tuesday afternoon, Samantha's sampler read "ACTIONS SPEAK LOUDER THA." The sewing hour was almost over when there was a gentle knock on the parlor door.

"Come in," said Grandmary, and Jessie came in dressed to leave for home. She curtsied quickly and waited for Grandmary to speak.

Samantha thought Jessie always looked elegant. She was so tall and held her head so high. Jessie looked especially grand today. She was wearing a light brown summer coat that came almost to the floor. But Samantha wondered why she was leaving so early.

"Yes, Jessie?" questioned Grandmary.

"Ma'am, I've just come to say I won't be coming back now," Jessie said.

Samantha almost jumped out of her chair. "Jessie! Why?" she asked.

Grandmary silenced her with a look that said children should be seen and not heard. She spoke to Jessie. "Very well, Jessie. I'd like to thank you for your service. You have been a great help and a pleasure to us. We shall miss you very much."

Samantha was horrified. What was Grandmary saying? How could she just let Jessie go away like that?

"You can see Hawkins for your pay," continued Grandmary. "There will be a bonus for you."

Jessie curtsied again. "Thank you, ma'am." Before she left she stopped to smile at Samantha. "Be very good, Miss Samantha. You know I'll miss you."

Samantha was too stunned to answer. She watched Jessie go. Then her words rushed out. "Grandmary, why is Jessie leaving? And why did you let her?"

Grandmary's eyes never moved from the lacework in her hands. "Please sit down, Samantha,"

Samantha almost jumped out of her chair.
"Jessie! Why?"

she said. "A young lady must not ask questions of her elders. This is Jessie's business."

Samantha sat down, but she could only fidget with her sewing. It seemed as if every stitch she put in her sampler had to be pulled out again. She didn't understand. Why would Jessie leave without explaining?

At last the sewing hour was over. Samantha curtsied quickly when Grandmary excused her. Then she rushed out of the parlor to find Mrs. Hawkins, the cook.

There was never any problem finding Mrs. Hawkins. She was always in the kitchen. And the kitchen was always filled with the wonderful smells of Mrs. Hawkins's cooking. Today she stood by the big wooden table in the center of the room, rolling pastry for meat pie. She wasn't surprised to see Samantha. The kitchen was one of Samantha's favorite places. She came there often to talk and to eat the treats Mrs. Hawkins saved for her.

"Hello, love," Mrs. Hawkins said. "Why are you rushing so? Sit down now and tell me what's the matter. You look like thunder."

Samantha flopped herself down on a chair. "Jessie's gone away," she said.

"Yes, dear, I know."

Mrs. Hawkins knew? Everybody knew but Samantha! She brushed away a fly that buzzed in from the open windows. "But why?" she asked. "Grandmary didn't even try to stop her!"

"Now, now, love. You must not fret about it," Mrs. Hawkins said. She took an onion from a bunch hanging by the door and began to peel it. "There are some things you just don't understand. Don't you think your Grandmary knows best?"

How could Samantha possibly know if Grandmary knew best? How could she know if anybody knew best? She didn't know what anybody knew!

She pushed back her chair and hurried from the kitchen to the butler's pantry. She hoped Hawkins would be there, and he was. Hawkins was whistling softly and polishing silver. He pulled out a chair for Samantha. He was used to her popping up in strange places. They had their best talks when Samantha followed him around on his jobs, waxing furniture, beating the carpets, or washing the windows in Grandmary's big house. Now Hawkins handed Samantha a polishing cloth. He knew how much easier it is to talk when your hands are busy.

Samantha rubbed at a sugar bowl. "Jessie's gone," she said.

"I know," said Hawkins. Samantha wasn't surprised.

"Nobody will tell me why," Samantha went on.

Hawkins smiled, and his eyes were understanding. But when he spoke, it didn't help much. "Believe me, Miss Samantha, Jessie's fine," he said. "I know it isn't easy, but sometimes, when you're young, you just have to trust."

Samantha didn't feel much like talking anymore. She pushed back the sugar bowl and cloth, straightened her chair, and slowly left the pantry. As she shuffled past the parlor, Grandmary called, "Samantha."

"Yes, ma'am?"

"I have been very pleased with your efforts these past weeks," Grandmary said. "If you go upstairs, you will find something on your bed."

For a minute Samantha forgot about Jessie's leaving. She even forgot to say thank you as she ran up the stairs two at a time. Inside her room, Samantha stopped short. There in the middle of her bed was a doll dressed in shining blue silk. She had a wide silk hat to match. Her soft china hands and face were rosy and delicate. "Oh, Lydia," Samantha whispered. She picked the doll up gently. Then she hugged her very close.

NIGHT VISIT

The next morning, Samantha brought Lydia to meet Nellie in the tunnel. But when she saw how Nellie's eyes glowed and how gently she touched Lydia's dress, Samantha wondered if she had been wrong to bring the doll. Nellie had never owned a doll, not even a simple doll, and certainly not a doll as beautiful as Lydia.

"It's all right if you play with her," Samantha said. "Look. Her hat can come off and her dress even has little buttons."

While Nellie cradled Lydia, Samantha told her what had happened.

"Jessie left, and nobody will tell me why," Samantha said.

Nellie didn't answer. She was buttoning the tiny buttons.

"I think I know, though," Samantha continued. "I think she's going to be an actress."

Nellie carefully removed Lydia's hat and turned it over in her hand.

"She'll be famous," Samantha went on. "And one day she'll come back here, and we'll go to see her. And she'll take you and me to meet all the actors and actresses. Only you and me, out of the whole town. Because we were her friends."

Nellie still had nothing to say. Now she was

looking at the doll's tiny leather shoes.

In the days that followed, Samantha came up with several reasons for Jessie's leaving. Maybe Jessie had gone to New Orleans with Lincoln, to be a singer there. Jessie had a beautiful voice. Or the President might have asked her to be a spy in Europe. She'd sew elegant clothes for kings and queens and learn their secrets. Or maybe her brother had been kidnapped and taken to South America, and Jessie was going to rescue him.

Then one day Nellie had a suggestion. "Maybe she's got a baby," Nellie said.

Samantha was startled. "Why would she do that?"

Nellie shrugged. "Lots of people do. They just like babies," she said.

Samantha had to agree. "Jessie loves babies."

"Well then?"

Samantha was annoyed. Nellie's idea wasn't half as exciting as any of hers. But it was too sensible to be ignored. "Why wouldn't Grandmary tell me if it was a baby?" asked Samantha.

Nellie shrugged again. "Grownups don't like to talk about babies coming."

Samantha had to agree. "I asked Grandmary about babies once, and she said it wasn't a proper subject for young girls."

Nellie nodded in understanding.

"I asked Mrs. Hawkins, and she said the stork brings babies. But she wouldn't talk about it anymore," Samantha continued.

"I don't think it's true anyway," said Nellie. "When my baby sister came, the midwife was at our building. My other sister and I had to go out with my uncle. When we got back, my baby sister was there and the midwife was fixing tea for my mother. But there wasn't any stork anywhere."

Samantha was puzzled. "What's a midwife?" she asked.

"She's a lady who visits whenever a new baby comes," Nellie answered. "My uncle said she brings the baby in her little black bag. But I looked in, and the bag was full of things like doctors have. There wouldn't be any room for a baby in there."

"Nellie, we've just *got* to find out what happened to Jessie," said Samantha. "If we just

knew where she lived, we could ask Lincoln.
He must know where she is."

"I know where she lives," said Nellie.

Samantha's eyes were wide with surprise.
"You do?"

Nellie nodded. "A woman across the street
from Jessie makes an herb tea that cures headaches.
One day Mrs. Ryland wanted some, so she sent me
home with Jessie to get it. I can show you."

Samantha hugged her. "Oh, Nellie, that's
perfect! Only we can't go in the daytime. They'd
stop us for sure. We'll go tonight. When everyone's
in bed, I'll sneak down the back stairs and meet
you right here in the tunnel. Look out your window
and watch my house. Grandmary always turns out
the gas lamps just before she goes to bed. That's
how you'll know it's all right for me to come down
and meet you."

Nellie agreed. She knew that no one at the
Ryland house would even notice if she went out
after she had finished her evening chores.

Samantha had always thought the nighttime was very quiet, but that night, noises seemed to come from everywhere. The crickets were making a terrible racket. The bushes and trees rustled as though they were hiding wild animals, and dogs barked all around. Samantha closed the back door carefully and hurried to the tunnel to find Nellie.

The two girls held hands and started out of the yard and up the street. As long as they were on familiar streets, where gas lamps glowed with a friendly light, they thought their adventure was grand and very exciting. But after they crossed the railroad tracks, the streets got dark and narrow. The houses were dark, too, and very small. Somewhere there was loud music and noisy laughter, and once in a while there was shouting. Nellie squeezed Samantha's hand so tightly that Samantha couldn't have let go if she'd wanted to. But she certainly didn't want to. She was just as frightened as her friend was. *Maybe we shouldn't have come at all,* she thought. But she didn't say that to Nellie. She wanted to be brave.

"Are you sure you know the way?" Samantha whispered.

"I—I think so." Nellie's voice was shaky. "It's not much farther now."

Samantha looked at the drab houses they were passing. Even in the dark she could tell there wasn't much grass in front, and there was very little room for flowers. "Why does Jessie live here?" she asked.

"This is the colored part of town," Nellie answered.

"You mean Jessie *has* to live here?" Samantha asked.

Nellie looked at her. Samantha was smart about so many things that Nellie was always surprised at what her friend didn't know. "Yes, of course," Nellie said.

"Why?" asked Samantha.

"I don't know," Nellie said. "It's just the way grownups do things." Her face lit up with relief. "There it is," she said. The soft glow of a kerosene lamp shone from a window, and the girls rushed to the wall beneath it. They huddled there for a minute, panting.

"Aren't you going to knock on the door?" Nellie whispered.

Samantha suddenly lost her nerve. "What if it's not the right house after all?" she said. "Or what if Jessie went away with Lincoln, and somebody else lives there now?"

"Well, we can look in the window," said Nellie. "I'll get down and you can get on my back. Then you can see in."

"No, I'm stronger," answered Samantha. "You get on my back."

Samantha got on her hands and knees. Nellie stepped carefully onto her back. She held tight to the windowsill and looked over. "Oh, Samantha," she whispered. "Jessie's there . . . and Lincoln, too, and . . . and . . ."

"What?"

"There's a cradle."

At just that moment Jessie looked up. She shrieked at the face she saw peering in at her. Nellie tried to duck, but she lost her balance and fell over, kicking Samantha in the ribs as she went. So it was a tangle of arms and legs and frightened faces that Lincoln found when he came outside the house. He laughed out loud.

Inside, Jessie brushed the girls' dresses.

It was a tangle of arms and legs and frightened faces that Lincoln found when he came outside the house.

"I declare, Miss Samantha, I think I'll spend the rest of my life straightening you up after mischief," she chuckled. "What on earth are you doing here at such a time of night? Where's Hawkins?"

The girls looked at one another shyly. Then Samantha spoke. "We came by ourselves, Jessie. We didn't know what had happened to you, and no one would tell us."

Jessie's smile melted and she put her arms around Samantha. "My poor child," she said. "I'm sorry. I never dreamed you'd worry. But you see, I'm fine." She stood back and smiled proudly. "And now, come see my treasure." She went to the cradle and lifted out a tiny blanketed bundle. She brought it over to the girls and announced, "This is Nathaniel."

Wrapped in the blanket was the tiniest person Samantha had ever seen. His skin was the same fine brown as his mother's, and his head was covered with soft black curls. His cheeks were so round and soft that Samantha couldn't resist reaching out to touch them. When his tiny pink mouth opened and closed, she was sure he smiled at her. "Oh, Jessie," she breathed. "He's beautiful."

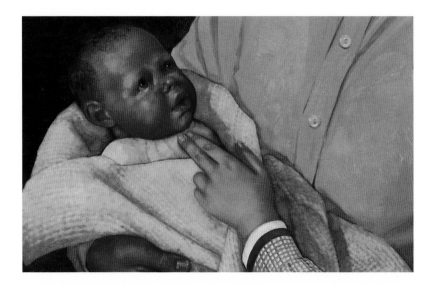

Jessie beamed and tucked the baby back in his cradle with a kiss. "But you see why I couldn't stay at your grandmother's," she said, turning back to the girls. "Lincoln's gone most of the time, working. I've got to be here to take care of Nathaniel. But don't worry, Miss Samantha. I'll come to see you often. And I'll bring Nathaniel, too." She hugged Samantha quickly. Then she hustled the girls to the door. "Now Lincoln is going to take you home. If your grandmother finds out you're gone, she'll have your hide and mine, too."

The way home seemed much shorter with

Lincoln's strong hands to guide them. Nellie and
Samantha crept into their houses without making a
sound. Samantha tiptoed quickly up the stairs and
back into her room. She hurried to unbutton her
shoes and take off her stockings. She hung her
dress in the tall wooden wardrobe, unbuttoned her
underwaist, and slipped her long ruffled nightgown
over her head. Her nightgown had never felt so soft
and warm. Her bed had never smelled so sweet or
been so welcome. She held Lydia very close and
fell asleep.

CHAPTER
SIX

A FINE
YOUNG LADY

 Two days later, Samantha tugged on the string of her tin-can telephone. She and Nellie had tied bells to both ends of the telephone, so that they could signal one another when they wanted to talk. But today Nellie didn't answer.

Samantha tugged again, but still there was no answer. She crawled through the tunnel. There was no sign of Nellie. Instead, Eddie Ryland stood there pulling gum out of his mouth in long strings and then stuffing it back in again.

"I know something you don't know," Eddie said. He looked pleased with himself, and that worried Samantha. She waited.

"Nellie is going away," Eddie said.

Samantha felt as though she'd been hit. "What are you talking about, Eddie?"

"Our driver's taking her back to the city. She's sick, and my mother says she's not strong enough to work. She's waiting in the kitchen. Mother says next time we'll get an immigrant woman who can last longer."

Samantha wanted more than anything to punch Eddie in the nose. But she knew she couldn't. She knew that even if she were a boy, she couldn't punch Eddie in the nose. Certainly a grown-up person would not punch Eddie in the nose. A grown-up person probably would not have reached out and shoved Eddie's chewing gum into his hair either. But Samantha did. After all, she was only nine, and that is only half grown-up. Then she rushed to her friend, leaving Eddie howling and trying to pull the sticky mess out of his curls.

In the Rylands' kitchen, Nellie sat on a wooden chair, swinging her legs and staring at her belongings. They were tied in a shawl at her feet.

"Nellie, are you sick?" Samantha asked.

Nellie looked up. "No, I'm not sick," she said.

48

"But I still cough sometimes. Mrs. Ryland is afraid I'll get sick and be a bother, so she's sending me back."

"But Nellie, will you have to go to work in the factory again? You'll get sick if you go back. And what will I do without you?"

Nellie had started to cry. "It'll be all right, Samantha. Really it will. Only I'll miss you so much."

Samantha couldn't stand to see Nellie crying. "Wait a minute, I'll be right back," she said. She dashed across the yard and into her own kitchen.

"Mrs. Hawkins!" Samantha cried breathlessly. "Mrs. Hawkins, they're sending Nellie away, and her family doesn't have enough food. We have to give them something."

Mrs. Hawkins would have been quick to help even without Samantha's begging. In a few minutes she had packed a basket with a pie and fruit, some food in tin cans, and a ham. Samantha ran back to the Rylands' kitchen carrying the basket—and something else. She put the basket at Nellie's feet. Then she placed Lydia in her arms.

"Here, Nellie. You take Lydia," Samantha said.

"Here, Nellie. You take Lydia," Samantha said.
"She'll be your friend."

50

"She'll be your friend." Samantha hugged Nellie and stayed with her until the Rylands' driver came.

Later that afternoon, Uncle Gard and Cornelia were having tea with Grandmary. Samantha was there, too, but she was not playing and laughing with Uncle Gard. She was sitting in her chair, working on her sampler, because even *that* was better than talking to grownups. Samantha was feeling very angry with grownups. Grownups took her friends away and never even told her why. So she sat and stabbed the needle at her sampler, and everyone wondered why Samantha was in such a bad mood.

Then suddenly, even before she knew she was going to, Samantha blurted out, "I know why Jessie left."

Grandmary looked surprised. "You do?"

"Yes. She has a baby," Samantha said.

Now Grandmary was really surprised. "How do you know that?" she asked.

"Nellie and I went to her house at night, and we saw." Samantha was sure Grandmary would punish her now.

But Grandmary looked more troubled than angry. "You were very wrong to do that, Samantha," she said.

"Well, you were very wrong not to tell me," Samantha answered. She was not feeling very respectful.

Grandmary took in her breath sharply. She looked at Uncle Gard and Cornelia for help. But they said nothing.

Grandmary put her teacup down and nodded slowly. "Yes, Samantha, I think you are right. I should have told you," she said.

The room was very quiet. Samantha felt pleased and relieved. "Well, can Jessie come back?" she asked.

"Now, Samantha, you know she has to take care of the baby."

"But she could bring him with her," said Samantha. "He wouldn't bother anybody."

Grandmary looked thoughtful. "Well, I hadn't thought about that. But I suppose if Jessie wants to, and Mrs. Hawkins doesn't object . . ." As if anyone could possibly imagine Mrs. Hawkins objecting to Nathaniel!

"Oh, thank you, Grandmary!" Samantha almost shouted. But Grandmary wasn't used to making mistakes, and she was feeling embarrassed. She changed the subject. "You don't have your doll today, Samantha. Are you tired of her already?"

Samantha looked down and felt her face turn hot. "No—no, I lost her."

"You *lost* her?" Grandmary was upset. "My dear Samantha, how are you ever going to grow into a proper young lady? I try and I try to give you a sense of value and you—"

"I think Sam's sense of value is just fine, Mother," Uncle Gard interrupted quietly. "She gave the doll to Nellie. Mrs. Hawkins told me."

Grandmary stopped short. She looked at Uncle Gard, and then she looked at Samantha. Then she nodded slowly. "Yes," she said. "Yes, I think Samantha's sense of value is just fine indeed."

Samantha ran to her grandmother.

"Grandmary, we've got to help Nellie's family. They don't have enough food and they don't have enough coal. Can we help them? Please?"

Grandmary's eyebrows went up, and then she threw back her head and laughed. "Yes, Samantha, yes! I guess if you care enough to give up your finest treasure, then we can find a way to help Nellie's family." She gave Samantha a proud smile. "You really are quite a fine young lady, Samantha Parkington," she said as she opened her arms to fold Samantha in a hug as warm as summer sunshine.

TO DAVID, RACHEL,
AND DANIEL, WHO KEEP
CHILDHOOD OPEN TO ME

Samantha
LEARNS A LESSON

BY SUSAN S. ADLER

NOTES AND KNEE BENDS

Something poked Samantha in the back. Samantha jumped slightly, but she didn't look up. She knew the signal. It was from Helen.

Helen Whitney had the desk behind Samantha's. Both desks were like all the other desks in the classroom at Miss Crampton's Academy for Girls. Their iron sides were molded in lacy swirls and curls. And one particular curl was just the right size for holding notes.

Talking in class was not allowed at Miss Crampton's, so when Helen had something to tell Samantha, she would write it on a small piece of paper. Then she would roll the paper up, stick it in the proper iron curl, and poke Samantha in the back with her pencil. Samantha would wait until Miss Stevens wasn't looking, and then drop her hand back and pull out the note. Once she caught her finger in the iron swirls and barely got it loose before Miss Stevens turned around. But usually the system worked wonderfully.

Now Samantha waited until the teacher's back was turned. She reached for the note. It said:

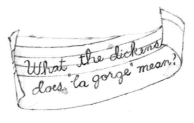

What the dickens does "la gorge" mean?

Samantha looked up quickly, squashed the note small, and shoved it into her pocket. It would be bad enough to be caught passing notes in school. She couldn't imagine what would happen if she were caught with a note that said *the dickens*. Didn't Helen have enough sense not to write almost-swear-words in school?

There wasn't enough time for Samantha to answer Helen's note. Miss Stevens had already finished writing a long list of French words on the

blackboard. Now she turned around and faced the class. And she looked straight at Helen.

"Helen, will you please tell us what *la gorge* means?" Miss Stevens asked.

Samantha tried to give Helen a clue. "A-a-ahemm," she cleared her throat rather loudly. Miss Stevens stared at her, then looked back at Helen.

Helen didn't answer, so Samantha tried again. She rubbed the back of her neck.

"Samantha, are you well?" asked Miss Stevens. She was looking at Samantha through gold-rimmed spectacles that seemed to see everything. She looked as if she had a pretty good idea of what was going on.

"Yes, ma'am," said Samantha softly. She folded her hands on her desk. Helen would have to answer on her own.

"Is it the neck?" squeaked Helen uncertainly.

"No, Helen, it is not," said Miss Stevens. She looked around the room. Edith Eddleton stretched her hand high in the air, and Miss Stevens called on her.

"*La gorge,*" said Edith smugly, "means the throat."

"That is correct," said Miss Stevens, and Edith gloated. Samantha could just imagine Edith keeping score in her head: "me—107; everyone else—0." Edith was smart, but not as smart as she thought she was. Probably no one on earth was as smart as Edith Eddleton thought she was.

The class was just finishing the list of words on the blackboard when the lunch bell rang. The girls stood beside their desks. They waited until Miss Stevens nodded for them to go and get their lunch boxes from the cloakroom. Then they filed quietly out the door.

The day was warm, so the girls could eat outside on the benches in the yard. Helen, Ida Dean, and Ruth Adams waited for Samantha at their usual spot. Samantha squirmed as she sat down next to them. Her legs itched from the long flannel underwear that was tucked under her stockings. But she had to wear it, whether the days were warm or cold. Grandmary said flannel

*The day was warm, so the girls could eat outside
on the benches in the yard.*

underwear kept children from getting consumption, and she insisted that Samantha put it on at the beginning of September.

"Do you think Miss Crampton will make us do arm stretches today?" Ida asked between bites of her chopped olive sandwich. Miss Crampton was Head of the Academy, and she was very serious about exercise. At one o'clock every day she came to the classroom to lead the girls in exercises. "If she makes us do fifty arm stretches, I'm going to faint," Ida added with a sigh.

"At least arm stretches are better than knee bends," answered Helen. "I hate knee bends. I think Miss Crampton is trying for the world record in knee bends."

"It could be worse," said Ruth. "At my cousin's school they have to practice swimming. But they don't have any water. They have to hang with big ropes around their waists. Then they have to kick and paddle. Just hanging in the air like that."

Ida looked at her in disbelief. "Oh, they never!" she gasped.

Ruth nodded importantly. "I swear it. They do." And she licked jelly neatly off her fingers.

The girls were quiet for a moment, all giving silent thanks for the swimming hole in Mount Bedford. At least they could learn to swim in *real* water. "Maybe knee bends aren't so bad after all," Ida finally said.

Samantha took a gingerbread cookie out of her lunchbox and grew quiet while the other girls talked on. Every time she had gingerbread, Samantha thought about Nellie. Samantha had given Nellie her first taste of gingerbread last summer, when Nellie worked next door at the Rylands' house. But Mrs. Ryland sent Nellie back to the city. Now Samantha missed her friend. She thought about Nellie every day. She remembered all the things Nellie had told her about her life in the city, and she worried.

Nellie had said her whole family—all five of them—lived in one room in a crowded building. There was only one window in the room, and the air always smelled bad. In the summer the room was very hot, and in the winter it was terribly cold. There was a little stove for cooking, but there was never enough coal to make the room warm. And

Nellie had said they were nearly always hungry, because there wasn't enough money.

Samantha remembered all the things Nellie had told her, and the gingerbread tasted dry in her mouth.

As she swallowed the last of her milk, Samantha's thoughts were jerked back to the schoolyard by the ringing of Miss Crampton's bell. She hurried to get in line with the other girls. They all marched back inside to face another afternoon beginning with Miss Crampton's knee bends.

CHAPTER
TWO
—
NELLIE

On Saturday morning Samantha was
getting dressed when there was a
sharp knock at her door. Elsa leaned
her head in. "You have company, miss," she said.
Elsa looked annoyed at having to bother with
Samantha's company. "Your grandmother said to
tell you it's a friend. She's in the parlor." Samantha
was surprised. She had lots of friends who came
to play, but Grandmary would never tell any of
them to wait in the parlor. The parlor was only for
grown-up visitors. Samantha hurried downstairs.
She stopped in the hall to straighten her dress, then
slowly opened the parlor door and looked around.
At first she thought the room was empty. Then she

saw a wide blue bow just peeking over the back of
the green velvet chair. That was enough.

"Nellie!" Samantha yelled. She ran around the
chair and hugged the girl who jumped up to meet
her. Nellie was laughing.

"Oh, Nellie, it's really you! You're all right!"
Samantha stood back and looked at her friend.
"Are you back at the Rylands'?" she asked.

"Oh, no, it's much better," Nellie said. Her
eyes were sparkling. "It was your grandmother,
Samantha. She did it. She talked to Mrs. Van Sicklen,
and Mrs. Van Sicklen hired my mother and father.

Dad will be her driver. He'll take care of the horses and the garden. Mam will cook and clean and do laundry. And Bridget and Jenny and I will help." Nellie bounced with excitement. She looked as if she had a grand surprise. "And guess what, Samantha? We get to *live* there! All of us! We really do! In the rooms over the carriage house. Isn't that wonderful?"

Samantha grabbed Nellie's hands and danced with her around the parlor. "Oh, Nellie! You'll live only two houses away. We can play every single day when I get home from school."

Nellie stopped. Only her eyes danced now. She leaned over as if to tell a secret. "Samantha," she said in an excited half-whisper, "I'm going to go to school, too. Mrs. Van Sicklen told your grandmother I could." Nellie jumped a little jump and clapped her hands. "What do you think of that?"

Samantha hugged her. "Oh, Nellie, that *is* wonderful. It's just wonderful! I'm so glad you're back!" Samantha swung Nellie around in a circle and then started toward the door. "Come on," she called, "maybe Mrs. Hawkins will give us some gingerbread!"

Monday morning Samantha led a strange parade down the hill, across Main Street, and into the Mount Bedford Public School. She walked tall and proud, dressed in her best gray dress. Nellie walked next to her, skipping little excited skips now and then. Jenny and Bridget, Nellie's little sisters, followed behind. They squeezed each other's hands and walked very quietly.

Bridget was seven and Jenny was six. They would both start in the first grade. They looked shy and scared as they tiptoed into their classroom.

Then Samantha led Nellie to the second grade classroom. Nellie would start there because she knew her letters and she could read a little, even though she had never been to school before. In the dim hallway, facing the tall oak door, Nellie looked frightened. She twisted her hand in her dress and looked at Samantha for help. "Everything will be fine, you'll see," Samantha said. "Remember, I'll meet you on the front steps when school's over."

Nellie took a deep breath and stepped into her

classroom. Samantha hurried out of the building and ran the two blocks to Miss Crampton's.

All day long Samantha worried about Nellie. During morning exercises she wished she had taught Nellie the Oath of Allegiance. She knew they would be saying it in the public school. Did Nellie know it? Did she know the hymns they would sing?

At lunchtime, as Samantha ate her watercress sandwich, she remembered the lard pails Nellie and her sisters had carried as lunchboxes. She wished she had looked inside. She wasn't sure they had enough to eat. At least she could have given them her cookies.

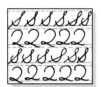 During penmanship class, Samantha practiced S's and Q's and thought that she should have stayed longer with Nellie. Would someone help her find the pencil sharpener? Would there be someone to show her where the bathroom was?

By three o'clock Samantha was almost bursting to know how Nellie had gotten along. She ran the two blocks to the public school and climbed the front steps two at a time. Jenny and Bridget began jumping up and down the minute they saw her. Both of them talked at once.

"There are thirty desks in our room, Samantha. I can count to thirty," Bridget said.

"I have my own desk," Jenny added.

"We put our lunches in the clock room," Bridget continued.

"No, Bridget, it's not a clock room, it's a *cloak* room," said Samantha.

"We have books, see?" Jenny held up three books strapped together with a leather belt.

"That's nice, Jenny," said Samantha. "But where's Nellie? Why isn't she here?"

The little girls looked at each other and shrugged. "We don't know. We haven't seen her."

Samantha looked around. All the other boys and girls were on their way home. Samantha saw Eddie Ryland pulling Carrie Wilson's hair ribbon off and running down the street with it. But there was no sign of Nellie. Where could she be?

Then Samantha saw her. Nellie was huddled by the bushes near the foot of the steps. She was sitting on her heels with her head in her hands. And she was crying.

The three girls ran down the steps and crouched next to Nellie. Jenny and Bridget began patting their sister's back and stroking her hair. Samantha put her arm around Nellie. "What is it? What's the matter?" she asked.

"I can't do it, Samantha," Nellie sobbed. "I'm too old to start school. I can't do it."

"But Nellie, what happened?"

"The children all laughed at me because I'm big and I'm just in second grade," said Nellie as she lifted her tear-stained face. "The teacher made me sit at the back of the room. And she got mad at me when I couldn't get the right answer. She asked me where the Atlantic Ocean was, and I was just so scared that I forgot. Then the children laughed even more." Nellie shuddered with a little sob. "They called me 'ragbag.' And one time when a boy passed my desk, he leaned over and whispered 'dummy.'" Nellie hid her face in her lap again. "Oh, Samantha, I can't go back tomorrow," she sobbed.

"Yes, you can, Nellie," Samantha said firmly. She was angry now. She was very angry. And when Samantha was angry, she was not likely to sit still.

"Nellie, do you know the way home by yourself?" Samantha asked. Nellie nodded. "Well then, you take Jenny and Bridget home. I have to do something. Dry your eyes. It's going to be all right. I promise you it's going to be all right."

Nellie rubbed her hand over her eyes and sniffed loudly. But she got up, took her sisters' hands, and started home. Samantha marched back to Miss Crampton's Academy.

MOUNT BETTER SCHOOL

Miss Stevens was at her desk. She was busy writing something, but she stopped when she saw Samantha. "Can I help you, Samantha?" she asked.

"Yes, Miss Stevens," answered Samantha. She did not know quite how to begin. At last she said, "I have a friend, and she's just started school. She's nine, but she never went to school because she had to work in a factory. She's in the second grade." Samantha stopped and watched Miss Stevens closely to see if she would think this was funny. But Miss Stevens didn't look as if she thought there was anything funny at all.

Samantha went on. "The children tease her and

the teacher is mean. She thinks my friend isn't very smart. But she *is* smart, Miss Stevens. She just needs help."

Miss Stevens nodded, so Samantha kept talking. "I could teach her, but I don't know what she needs to learn." She looked at Miss Stevens hopefully. "Can you help us?"

Miss Stevens looked thoughtful. "You are a very good friend, Samantha. I think you will be a good teacher, too. Come sit down."

Samantha sat on the chair next to her teacher's desk, and Miss Stevens went to a bookshelf at the side of the room. She came back with four books. "These are the second grade books," she said. "There's a speller, a reader, an arithmetic book, and a geography book." Miss Stevens began writing in the books with a pencil. "I'm marking parts in each of them. Do you think you can help your friend learn them?"

"Yes, Miss Stevens," Samantha said.

"Good," Miss Stevens replied. "Now, stop and see me after school on Friday. Tell me how much your friend has done, and I will help you plan for the following week. It's going to mean quite a bit of work, Samantha. Do you think you can do it?"

"Oh, yes. We can do it!" Samantha stood up, reached for the books, and dashed out of the classroom.

Samantha ran most of the way home. She was so eager to get started that she almost forgot to curtsy when she burst into Grandmary's sitting room. She remembered and bobbed quickly, just in time to avoid her grandmother's frown.

"Grandmary, may I start a school?" asked Samantha in a rush.

Even though Grandmary was used to the unexpected from Samantha, she could still be surprised. She raised an eyebrow and looked at her granddaughter. "Why, Samantha, are you quite sure you've learned all that Miss Stevens has to teach you?"

Samantha tried to explain. "Grandmary, I want to start a school for Nellie. She's having a terrible time at the public school. The teacher is mean to her, and the children tease her because she's just in second grade. But if I helped her, she could move up to the third grade really fast. I just know she could."

Grandmary thought for a minute before she answered. "I'm glad that you are willing to help Nellie," Grandmary said. "But you must not take up too much of her time, Samantha. Nellie has duties at the Van Sicklens' house, and I know you would not want her to neglect them."

"I won't take too much time, I promise," said Samantha. "And we'll be so quiet, you won't even know we're here." A little smile crept around Grandmary's mouth, and Samantha knew she had won.

"Very well," said Grandmary. "I guess it won't do any harm."

"Thank you, Grandmary," said Samantha as she hugged her grandmother quickly. Then she hurried out of the room to get her school ready.

It was past four o'clock when Samantha went into the Van Sicklens' backyard looking for Nellie. Samantha couldn't see anyone around, but she could hear someone in the laundry room. She peeked inside and saw Nellie ironing clothes. Nellie worked at a table in the middle of the room. Next to her, three irons sat on a small coal stove.

Nellie was sweating with the heat. She put the iron she was using back on the stove and picked up a hot one before she noticed Samantha. Her face brightened when she saw her friend.

"Can you come over to my house?" asked Samantha.

"Oh, not now," Nellie said as she wiped her face with the corner of her apron. "I have to finish the ironing first. But I'm pretty near done." She looked down at her basket. "I can come in about a half-hour."

"All right," Samantha said. "I'll wait for you on my back steps." She walked back to her house and sat with a book until she saw Nellie coming through the hedge.

Nellie was carrying Lydia, the beautiful doll that Samantha had given her. Lydia was no longer quite so fine. Her dress was wrinkled and worn because she had been held so often. Her hair was mussed because Nellie hugged her so tightly at night. Her china hands and face were dirty because Nellie took her with her wherever she could. Samantha looked at Lydia and knew she had been loved. "Come on, Nellie. I have something to

79

show you," she said.

Together, the two girls went inside. In the hallway next to the kitchen, Samantha opened a door that led to a curving stairway. She started up, and Nellie followed. The stairs ended on the second floor, at the back of Grandmary's house. Samantha opened another door. The steps were narrower now.

They ended in the attic. Samantha led the way down a narrow hall, past Elsa's room and Jessie's sewing room, to a third stairway. These steps were very steep, and sunlight poured down from above them.

As the girls climbed, Nellie's heart beat faster. She knew where they were now. Samantha was taking her to the small tower that rose above her house and made it look like a palace among the houses of Mount Bedford. Nellie held her breath as she followed Samantha up.

And suddenly they were there—in a tiny room above the world. There was a window in each of the four walls, and Nellie hurried to peer out of each one in turn. She could see all the way down the hill to School Street. She could see the Rylands' house and the Van Sicklens'. And she could see over the trees on the hill. Nellie had never been up so high before. She thought it felt like flying.

When she turned around, Nellie saw that the room was special inside, too. Samantha's small blackboard was there, standing on wooden legs like an easel. There were cushions to sit on and books stacked neatly against one wall. And there was a small jar of dried white beans.

Nellie was amazed. "Samantha, what . . . ?"

"Here, sit down. We're going to get you out of the second grade, Nellie. Put Lydia on the window seat and let's get started." Samantha opened a book to the place Miss Stevens had marked. "Why don't you start reading there, and when you come to a word you don't know, I'll write it on the blackboard so you can practice it."

Nellie read two pages and Samantha wrote eleven words on the blackboard. Nellie copied them in her copybook to take home and study.

Next they worked on penmanship. Samantha thought this might be difficult for Nellie. She remembered how hard it had been to make her own letters small enough, and how she had worked

Samantha opened a book to the place Miss Stevens had marked.

to get all the curls in the right places. But Nellie was fascinated by the letters. She loved the fancy look of them. Even though her first letters were crooked, she kept trying and trying to make them beautiful. Finally it was Samantha who said it was time to stop. They would have to go on to arithmetic.

Samantha spilled some beans out of the jar and onto the floor. She began arranging them in rows. "All right, Nellie, here are seven beans and here are five," she said. "Now, if you add them together—"

"Twelve," Nellie interrupted.

Samantha looked up, startled. She moved more beans into place. "Fourteen and nine," she said.

"Twenty-three," said Nellie, without bothering to count the beans.

Samantha scooped the beans back into the jar and said, "Seventeen and fifteen."

"Thirty-two," Nellie answered promptly.

Samantha sat back on her heels and stared at Nellie. "How did you know that?"

Nellie shrugged. "Lots of times in the city I did the shopping for Mam. I usually had just about a dollar, and I had to get food for all of us. I had to know how many pennies things cost. I had to know how many pennies I had left. And I had to know fast."

Samantha nodded slowly. She didn't want to think about Nellie counting pennies for food. She shoved the bean jar into a corner. "It's getting too late to look at the geography book now. We'll have to save that for another day," she said.

As the girls were stacking the books and getting ready to leave, Samantha had a thought. "You know, Nellie," she said, "we should have a name for our school. I think we should call it the Mount Better School." Her smile had mischief in it as she looked at Nellie. "We've got better students than the Mount Bedford School."

A grin flashed across Nellie's face. "We've got better teachers, too," she said.

C H A P T E R

F O U R

—

THE CONTEST

The next morning, Miss Crampton made an announcement. "The Mount Bedford Ladies Club will be sponsoring the Young People's Speaking Contest again this year. The contest will be held on October fifth in the Mount Bedford Opera House. This year's subject is 'Progress in America,'" she said.

"Students from Lessing's Boys School and from the public elementary school will compete in the contest," Miss Crampton continued. "Our own Academy has been asked to send two girls to take part. In order to choose those two girls, we shall have a contest of our own three weeks from today. Each of you will prepare and present a speech.

Miss Stevens and I shall choose the two best speeches."

"Think very carefully about progress in America," Miss Crampton went on. "Think of all the inventions that have changed our lives—the telephone, the steam engine, electric lights, and so many more. Talk to your parents and read books to get ideas. You have just three weeks to work on your speeches. You should begin today. And remember, I expect excellence."

By the time Miss Crampton finished, all the girls were thinking hard. And by lunchtime everyone was buzzing about the speaking contest.

"If you win," said Helen, "the mayor gives you the medal. Right up on the stage with everybody watching."

"It wouldn't matter if the *President* gave me a medal," said Ida glumly. "I get so nervous in front of people, I can hardly remember my name. I could never give a speech in public."

"You get your name in the paper if you win, too," Helen added.

"I would probably just faint and fall off the stage onto the mayor," said Ida. "And my parents would be so embarrassed, they'd have to leave town."

"I don't get nervous," said Ruth, "but I don't know enough big words to win. Judges always like big words."

"I'm going to keep smelling salts in my pocket," said Ida. "Remember them if I faint."

"Samantha's going to win," said one of the other girls. "Her essays are always the best, and she won't be scared on the stage."

Samantha shrugged modestly. "I wish I *could* win," she said. She knew she would certainly try. Wouldn't it be wonderful to be up on that stage and feel that medal in her hand?

"Edith Eddleton might win, though." It was Ruth speaking. Ruth was Samantha's friend, but she was an honest friend. "Edith knows more big words than the rest of us put together. And she's not scared of anything."

The other girls groaned. Helen made a face.

"Ruth," she said, "just be quiet and eat your sandwich."

At three o'clock, Nellie and her sisters waited for Samantha on the front steps of Mount Bedford Public School. This afternoon there were no tears.

"How was it, Nellie?" called Samantha as the three bounded down the steps.

"It wasn't too bad," answered Nellie. Bridget took Samantha's hand, and the girls started home.

"Did they tease you?" Samantha asked.

"They did some," said Nellie, trying to slow Jenny down. "But I didn't mind so much. The teacher mostly left me alone."

"Can you come to Mount Better School today?" asked Samantha.

Nellie looked uncertainly at Samantha. "I have to clean the parlor and sweep the mats," she said. "But if I get the table set right away, I can come for a little while before I have to serve dinner."

Just then Edith Eddleton came riding past on her bicycle. She looked at the girls and stopped. "Samantha Parkington, does your grandmother know you're walking home with *servant* girls?"

*"Samantha Parkington, does your grandmother know
you're walking home with **servant** girls?" Edith asked.*

Samantha was shocked. "What are you talking about?"

Edith was only too glad to go on. "Those are Mrs. Van Sicklen's servants. I know *my* mother doesn't want *me* to spend time with them. But then, I guess some people just aren't very particular." And Edith climbed back on her bicycle and pedaled away.

Nellie's face got very red. For once Samantha was speechless. She grabbed Bridget's hand tightly and marched up the sidewalk with long, angry steps. "You know, Nellie," Samantha finally said, "Edith Eddleton is even nastier than Eddie Ryland!"

That evening, Samantha had dinner with Grandmary. Samantha always loved the glitter of the silver and the crystal in the dining room. She loved the little silver bell Grandmary let her ring to tell Mrs. Hawkins to clear the table and bring dessert. She loved the special grown-up time she shared with Grandmary.

Of course, such a grown-up dinner wasn't easy. Samantha had to use her very best manners. She sat very straight and kept her napkin in her lap. She tilted her soup spoon away from her in her soup plate. She never spilled or dropped a crumb. She kept her elbows close to her sides, and she tried not to speak until she was spoken to.

Samantha waited until Grandmary asked her about school before she told about the speaking contest. "What do you think is the best sign of progress in America, Grandmary?" Samantha asked.

Grandmary paused for a moment. "First of all, Samantha," she said, "I think it is a mistake to assume that change means progress. The world got along quite well without all these new inventions and machines. Many of them have caused more confusion than they're worth."

Grandmary paused again. "Still," she said, "I think you'd have to say that the telephone has been of some help. Of course, it will never take the place of a courteous letter. But I think it does help Mrs. Hawkins when she orders meats and groceries. And it is a comfort if we should ever need the doctor or the fire department. Yes, I think I'd say the telephone is a useful invention."

Samantha had something else she wanted to talk about. But once again she had to wait until Grandmary noticed and asked, "Is something bothering you, Samantha?"

"Grandmary, why isn't Edith Eddleton allowed to play with Nellie?" Samantha asked.

Grandmary looked surprised. "Why, Samantha," she said. "Edith is a young *lady.*"

Samantha thought that was ridiculous. But all she said was, "You let me play with Nellie."

"You are *helping* Nellie," said Grandmary, "not playing with her. There is a difference."

Samantha was quiet. She didn't like the difference.

PROGRESS

Samantha was delighted that Uncle Gard came to visit on Saturday. She was even more pleased to see that he had not brought his friend Cornelia with him. That meant that after tea with Grandmary, Samantha could have him all to herself.

The net was set up for lawn tennis. Samantha served the ball over the net. Uncle Gard dived for it and hit it back. Samantha swung her racquet and missed.

"Uncle Gard," Samantha called as she brought the ball back and moved closer to the net, "I need to know about progress. I need to know for the speaking contest. Two girls from Miss Crampton's can enter. The winner gets a gold medal. Oh, Uncle Gard, I really want to win. Can you help me?"

Uncle Gard whistled. "That's a pretty big order. What do you need to know?"

"What's the best invention?" Samantha asked.

Her uncle thought a minute. "Well, electric lights are important, Sam. They make a big difference at night. And more and more people are getting them. I expect someday people will just have electric lights and we won't need gas lamps at all. And what about the automobile? Now, that's an important invention. People can go anywhere in automobiles."

"That's silly, Uncle Gard," said Samantha. "You can't go anywhere far away from a drugstore or you won't be able to get gasoline."

"Well, that's not a problem," said Uncle Gard. "Just take enough gasoline with you."

"And you can't go anywhere on a rainy day," said Samantha. "Automobiles get stuck in the mud."

"Have a heart, Sam," laughed Uncle Gard. "I thought you *liked* automobiles."

"I do," said Samantha as she got ready to hit the ball again. "But they're just not as much fun as horses."

"Why not?"

Samantha reached high and sent the ball sailing. "You can't feed carrots to an automobile!"

For two weeks, Samantha worked hard to learn about progress in America. She read books about new inventions. She took notes about the ideas she got from talking to different people. Mrs. Hawkins said the best invention was the gas stove because it didn't get full of ashes like a coal stove, and you didn't have to keep coals hot all night and all summer. She said that was progress. And Hawkins told Samantha about factories. He said factories were the most important sign of progress in America because there was no end to what they could make. He said they made things fast and they made things cheap. And he said that meant there were more

things for more people all over the country. That
started Samantha thinking.

Every afternoon Samantha and Nellie had
school in the tower room. Samantha wrote parts
of her speech in her copybook and read them aloud
to see how they sounded. Then she put the words
a different way and read them aloud again. Nellie
worked on reading, geography, and spelling. But
she knew how much Samantha wanted to win the
speaking contest, and she tried not to disturb her.

One afternoon when Nellie was walking home
with Samantha, they saw Edith Eddleton standing
on the sidewalk with Clarisse Van Sicklen. And
Clarisse and Edith saw them. "There's Samantha
Parkington keeping company with the servants
again," said Edith. She spoke very loudly. "Do you
suppose she's practicing to be a washwoman?"

Clarisse answered just as loudly, "Oh, no. I think
Nellie is teaching her how to speak for the contest."

"Well, of course, that's it," said Edith. "Maybe

we should all take lessons." And Edith and Clarisse
snickered loudly.

Samantha ignored them and took Nellie's hand.
But when they had walked on and could still hear
the girls laughing behind them, Samantha said
through clenched teeth, "Oh, Nellie, I wish girls
were allowed to fight. I most surely do."

Later that afternoon, when Samantha and
Nellie were working in Mount Better School, they
needed more pencils. Samantha went downstairs to
the library to get one from Grandmary's desk. On
her way back she heard voices in the parlor. Even
without looking at the calling cards on the hall table,
Samantha knew who was visiting Grandmary. She
recognized Mrs. Eddleton's high, shrill voice and
Mrs. Ryland's rasping one. And she thought she
heard Nellie's name.

Samantha moved closer to the door and peeked
through a crack. Mrs. Eddleton was speaking. "Well,
the entire neighborhood is simply shocked," she said.

Mrs. Ryland said, "Imagine bringing that
whole ragged family to live right here, right in our
neighborhood. I just don't know what got into Mrs.
Van Sicklen."

"Actually, it was my idea," said Grandmary calmly as she poured the tea. "I urged Mrs. Van Sicklen to give them a home. Their life in the city was quite dreadful." She passed the tea to her guests. "I believe Mrs. Van Sicklen is quite pleased with them. They are all good workers."

The two visitors looked a little embarrassed, but Mrs. Eddleton continued, "My Edith says they are simply filthy, practically in rags."

"They are poor, of course," answered Grandmary. "But I have always found them as clean as any children, and surprisingly well mannered." Grandmary's back was very straight. Samantha recognized the frosty look in her eye that should have warned the visitors to be careful. But the visitors were too busy talking to notice.

Then Mrs. Ryland asked, "Do you really think it's wise to let Samantha spend so much time with them?"

"I believe Samantha is doing them a great deal of good," said Grandmary. "And it is our duty to do good where we can." She put her teacup down. "Would you care for more tea, ladies?" she asked in a voice that was more polite than friendly.

*Grandmary had the frosty look in her eye
that should have warned the visitors to be careful.*

Samantha turned and hurried back up the hall. Suddenly she wanted to be close to Nellie.

After lunch on Thursday, all the girls in Miss Crampton's Academy filed quietly into the assembly room. They stood in front of their chairs until they had sung a hymn and said a prayer. Then they sat down with their backs straight and their hands folded in their laps. There was no whispering even before Miss Crampton began speaking.

"As you know, two girls from this Academy will represent all of us at the Speaking Contest tomorrow evening," Miss Crampton said. "Today, Miss Stevens and I will choose those two girls. They will be the two girls who give the best speeches about progress in America."

Even with her hands folded, Samantha managed to cross her fingers. She took deep breaths to steady herself.

Miss Crampton continued. "I know that everyone in Miss Stevens's class has worked very hard on a speech. And I know we are all very eager to hear the results of this hard work. So I will say nothing more. Helen Whitney, will you please come forward?"

Helen walked up, curtsied, and gave her speech. Then each of the other girls in Samantha's class spoke. Some of their voices were shaky. Ida Dean spoke so softly, the audience could barely hear her. But she didn't faint.

At last Samantha's turn came. She was the last girl to speak. Her voice was clear and steady.

"Factories in Modern America," she began. "American factories are the finest in the world. They are true signs of our progress. It used to take many hours to make a pair of shoes or a table by hand. Now machines can make hundreds of shoes and hundreds of tables in just a few hours. And they make thread and cloth, toys and bicycles, furniture, and even automobiles. These things cost less money than they used to because they are made by machines. So now more people can buy the things they want and the things they need. That is progress. Truly, we could not go forward into the twentieth century without our factories and without our machines.

They are the greatest sign of progress in America."

There was applause in the room. Miss Stevens nodded in approval. Samantha beamed as she walked back to her seat.

Miss Crampton looked immensely pleased as she stepped to the front of the room. "All of our young ladies have done a splendid job," she said. "I am proud of each one of them. And now, it gives me great pleasure to announce our winners. Will Miss Samantha Parkington please step forward."

Samantha rose and walked to the front of the room again. Miss Crampton handed her an award. The certificate was crisp and smooth in her hand. She felt her heart swell with pleasure as she heard the applause around her.

When the clapping stopped, Miss Crampton announced the other winner. It was Edith Eddleton.

CHAPTER SIX

WINNERS

In Mount Better School that afternoon, Nellie watched proudly as Samantha pinned her award to the wall. "Can I hear your speech, Samantha?" Nellie asked. There was no doubt in Nellie's mind that her friend's speech would be the best ever written since Abraham Lincoln's.

Samantha cleared her throat and used her most proper voice. She repeated her speech just as she had at the Academy, remembering with a thrill the applause that had followed it. She finished proudly and then looked at Nellie for the praise she was sure would be coming.

But Nellie was staring at the floor and running

her finger along the edge of the cushion.

"Well?" asked Samantha.

"It's very nice," said Nellie in a voice that said it really wasn't nice at all.

Samantha felt hurt. "What's the matter with it?" she asked.

"It's very nice. It's just . . . well, it's just not very true," said Nellie.

"What do you mean?"

"I used to work in a factory, Samantha. It's not like that."

Nellie *had* worked in a factory. Samantha had almost forgotten that. "Well, what's a factory like, then?" she asked.

Nellie was quiet. She was remembering things she didn't want to remember. "I worked in a big room with other kids," she said finally. "Twenty others, I guess. But that didn't make it fun. We couldn't play. We couldn't even talk. The machines were too noisy. They were so noisy that when I got home at night my ears were buzzing and it was a long time before I could hear anything. We had to go to work at seven in the morning, and we worked until seven at night. Every day but Sunday."

Nellie continued, "I worked on the machines that wound the thread. There were hundreds of spools. We had to put in new ones when the old ones got full, and we tied the thread if it broke. We had to stand up all the time. I got so tired, Samantha. My back hurt and my legs hurt and my arms got heavy. The machines got fuzz and dust all over everything. It was in the air, and it got in my mouth and made it hard to breathe."

Nellie was quiet again. Then she went on. "The room was awful hot in summer. But it was worse in winter because there wasn't any heat. Our feet nearly froze. We couldn't wear shoes."

Samantha was shocked. "You couldn't wear shoes?" she asked.

"We had to climb on the machines to change the spools, and shoes could make us slip. The machines were so strong, they could break your hand or your foot or pull a finger off as easy as anything. We all had to have our hair short. If your hair was long, the machines could catch it and pull it right out. They just kept winding. Once I saw that happen to a girl. She was just standing there, and then suddenly she was screaming and half her head was bleeding. She almost died."

Nellie was running her finger along the edge of the cushion again. "They paid us one dollar and eighty cents a week." She looked straight at her friend. "That's why thread is so cheap."

Samantha stared at Nellie. She couldn't move. She felt numb and cold, but her scalp was tingling and her arms had a strange ache in them.

The Mount Bedford Opera House was used for most of the town's special events. It served Mount Bedford for everything from roller-skating parties to concerts. On the evening of the Young People's Speaking Contest it was filled with wooden chairs.

The contest speakers sat on the stage, facing parents and friends from all over town. Grandmary sat in the second row, wearing a gray silk dress and looking calm and stately. Nellie sat with her mother near the back of the room. She looked shy and out of place.

As the president of the Mount Bedford Ladies Club stepped to the front of the stage, smiling and bobbing her head, the room grew quiet. She welcomed everyone, introduced the speakers, and told what schools they represented. Then it was time for the speeches.

One of the boys from Lessing's School told about a new building that was twenty stories high. He said that from now on, all cities would be different because of it. Another boy talked about automobiles, and someone spoke about electric lights. A girl from the public school talked about medicine. She said people didn't get sick as much as they used to. Then it was Edith Eddleton's turn.

Edith walked to the front of the stage like an army general. She paused for a moment with her head a little to one side. Then she boomed out her speech in a voice meant to reach the Opera House doors and beyond.

"We are indeed fortunate to live in this age of progress. Progress is the great American adventure. In the old days, a man had to work all day and all night to support himself and his family. But now, in modern America, great machines can be a great benefit to everyone. Now everyone can have all he needs without a difficult struggle. Fortunes can be made now as never before. Now, with the help of machines, anyone can become wealthy. What a great opportunity man has in the twentieth century. Are we not fortunate to live in this great age of progress?"

Everyone clapped loudly as Edith returned to her chair in triumph. She sat down, smoothed her dress, and smiled at Samantha.

Then Samantha heard her name called. She walked to the front of the stage calmly. She didn't look at Miss Crampton and Miss Stevens. She knew what they were expecting her to say. But she had learned something more about factories from Nellie, and now she had something else to say. Samantha stood tall and looked straight ahead. In her mind she could hear the words she had been practicing ever since her last lesson in Mount Better School.

"Americans are very proud of being modern," Samantha began. "We are proud of our progress. We are proud of the machines in our factories because they make so many new things for us. But Americans are proud of being truthful, too. If we were truthful, we would say that the factory machines make things fast and cheap, but they are dangerous, too. They can hurt the children who work in the factories. The machines can break their arms. They can cut off their fingers. They can make children sick. And children who work in factories don't have time to play or go to school. They are too tired." Samantha spoke calmly and clearly. She had discovered something. She had discovered that it is easy to talk to people, even to many people, if you really believe what you are saying.

"If our factories can hurt children, then we have not made good progress in America," Samantha

Samantha had discovered that it is easy to talk to people,
even to many people, if you really believe what you are saying.

110

continued. "And I believe Americans want to be good. I believe we want to be kind. And if we are kind, I believe we will take care of the children. Then we can truly be proud of our factories and our progress."

As Samantha walked back to her chair at the end of her speech, there was a long silence. Grandmary looked a little shocked. How could Samantha have known about such things? Then Grandmary looked back at Nellie. Nellie was sitting with her back straight and her eyes shining. And Grandmary understood. She understood a great deal. A proud smile spread across her face and she began to applaud. Her applause joined the clapping that began all over the room and grew into a long, loud roar of approval.

Edith Eddleton looked rather like a snowman that had been left too long in the sun.

The next time Samantha and Nellie sat in Mount Better School, it was not for a lesson. It was for a celebration. Samantha's first-prize medal hung from its blue ribbon on the schoolroom wall.

The girls were eating cookies and little cakes with pink frosting. Mrs. Hawkins had made them a whole pitcher of lemonade. They sat on cushions, with napkins spread on their laps, feeling very pleased with themselves.

Nellie sighed happily as she finished a cookie. She leaned back against the wall. "I'm glad we're celebrating today, Samantha. Something nice happened to me, too."

"Oh?" said Samantha, eager to share her friend's good news. "What?"

Nellie smiled shyly. "I moved to third grade."

Samantha jumped up, spun around, and clapped her hands. "Nellie, that's wonderful! That's just wonderful!" Then she stopped and looked at her friend. Nellie didn't look as happy as she should. "You didn't tell me right away, Nellie. What's wrong?" asked Samantha.

Nellie looked down at her napkin. Then she looked back at Samantha. "I have the desk next to Eddie Ryland."

Samantha's eyes grew wide and she sank back to the floor. "Ooohh, Nellie," she said with feeling. Both girls were quiet for a minute. Then Samantha pushed the cookies away and reached for a book. "Hurry up and finish your lemonade. We've got to start studying. You've got to move up to the head of the class!"

TO LILIANA, CECILIA,
AND SUSANA

Samantha's
SURPRISE

By Maxine Rose Schur

CHRISTMAS WISHES

"Wait, Samantha! I want to give you this." Samantha's friend Ida pressed a red envelope into her hand.

Samantha pulled off her mittens, tore open the flap, and drew out a card shaped like a Christmas stocking and edged with paper lace. It said:

*Miss Ida Dean requests
the pleasure of your company
at a Christmas Party
to be held at
six o'clock in the evening
Thursday, December 22
R.S.V.P.*

117

"Ooh, Ida," Samantha squealed. Her breath made little clouds in the chilly December air.

"I hope you can come," Ida said. "My brother is going to do magic tricks, and we'll play ladies' ring and charades!"

"Oh, it sounds wonderful!" Samantha said. "Ida, I think this is going to be the best Christmas ever!"

"Me, too," Ida agreed. "Especially if I get a new pair of ice skates. But do you know what I really want?"

"A dollhouse?" Samantha guessed.

"No."

"A sled?"

"No."

"A stereoscope?"

stereoscope

"No. A dog," Ida said. "A real cocker spaniel puppy!"

"Puppies are so cute! Do you think you'll get one?" Samantha asked.

"I don't know. I've asked and asked, though," Ida replied. "What are you hoping for?"

Samantha sighed. "What I really want is the doll I saw at Schofield's Toy Store," she said.

"I want that doll more than anything in the world!"

"What's she like?" Ida wondered.

"She's beautiful," Samantha replied. "She's dressed all in pink, even her shoes, and in her hand there's a tiny little—"

"Let's go look!" Ida interrupted.

The two girls raced down the street. As they ran, snowflakes swirled around them, clinging to their knitted mittens, resting in their hair, and brushing their cheeks like small, quick kisses.

At Schofield's Toy Store, the girls pressed their noses to the cold glass window. "There she is!" Samantha breathed. She pointed to a group of dolls that seemed to be dancing. They twirled around a taller doll who wore a lacy pink dress, pink pantalettes, and pink slippers. The doll held a tiny wooden soldier that looked just like the Nutcracker in the ballet.

"I love that Nutcracker doll," Samantha said.

"Well, do you think your grandmother will give it to you?" Ida asked.

"No . . ." Samantha answered slowly, looking down at her wet black boots. "I don't think so. I haven't asked her."

"I love that Nutcracker doll,"
Samantha said.

120

"You haven't *asked?*" Ida was puzzled. "Why not?"

"I just can't."

"What do you mean you *can't?*" Ida's voice rose. "Why can't you?"

"Because of Lydia," Samantha replied, remembering the beautiful doll that had been in Schofield's window last summer. Samantha had wanted that doll so much that Grandmary had bought it for her.

"You mean because you gave Lydia away?" Ida asked.

Samantha nodded.

"I would never, ever give a doll away. Especially a doll my grandmother had given to me!" Ida declared.

"But I gave Lydia to my friend Nellie. She had never owned a doll in her life. Not ever!"

"Oh." Ida paused. Then she added, "Well, now *you* don't have a doll. So why don't you ask your grandmother for this one?"

Samantha took one last look at the doll in the window, then shook her head. "I just don't think Grandmary would buy me another doll so soon.

She would probably think it was a terrible extravagance."

"But you should ask her anyway," Ida insisted as they walked toward Chestnut Street. "After all, the worst she can say is no."

"Maybe. Maybe I could ask her," Samantha said, more to herself than to Ida. They'd reached the corner, and Ida raced off into the snowflakes.

"Good-bye, Samantha," she called.

"See you tomorrow!" Samantha shouted back. She dodged a coal wagon, then ran up Chestnut Street to Grandmary's house.

Samantha let herself in the big front door and was immediately welcomed by the sweet, warm smell of just-baked sugar cookies. She followed the delicious scent to the kitchen. There was Mrs. Hawkins, the cook, stirring a pitcher of hot cocoa.

"Heavens, child! You're a sorry sight. Come, take off those cold, wet things." Mrs. Hawkins helped Samantha out of her wet coat and snow-caked boots, then sat her by the warm oven. "There, that's better," Mrs. Hawkins cooed, bringing Samantha the plate of sugar cookies.

"Get good and warm now. Here, I've made your hot cocoa just the way you like it—with lots of cinnamon."

Samantha ate a sugar cookie and took sips of the cocoa. When she felt warm inside and out, she said, "Mrs. Hawkins, Christmas is only two weeks away."

"That it is, Samantha, and it seems I'll never get everything done."

Samantha reached into her pocket and took out a folded piece of paper. She smoothed it open and said, "Look! I've made a design we can use for the gingerbread house."

Mrs. Hawkins squinted at the paper. "Oh, where did I put my spectacles?" she asked, searching around the table.

Samantha handed Mrs. Hawkins her glasses, which had been lying on top of the breadbox.

"Thanks, love. I seem to be forever looking for them," Mrs. Hawkins said, setting them on her nose. "Now, let's see." She studied the drawing silently for a few moments, then remarked, "It's cleverly planned, Samantha, but how *big* are you

123

expecting this gingerbread house to be?"

"About two feet across and two feet high."

"Two feet high! And you're sure this isn't a gingerbread train station?" Mrs. Hawkins teased.

"It *is* rather big," Samantha admitted, "but it's got to hold up a lot of things. We'll use taffy sticks for pillars and caramel squares for the doors. Cinnamon drops make the best chimney bricks, and for the drawbridge we can use licorice ropes!"

"My!" Mrs. Hawkins said. "It certainly sounds fancy."

"But we can do it—I know we can. Don't you think so, Mrs. Hawkins?" Samantha asked.

Mrs. Hawkins looked over the drawing again. "Yes, Samantha, I do believe that with a lot of ingredients, and quite a bit of time, and just a pinch of luck, we can make this house."

"Oh, I knew you'd say yes, Mrs. Hawkins. Thank you so much!" Samantha cried, jumping up and giving her a hug. "Let's do it Saturday!"

CHAPTER
TWO
—

PRESENTS AND A PARTY DRESS

 Samantha went up to her bedroom, closed the door, and turned the big brass key to lock it. Then she pulled her chair into the closet and climbed up on it. From the top of the chair she could just reach the big pink hatbox on the highest shelf. She brought it down and set it carefully on her bed.

The hatbox was Samantha's Christmas box. It held all the presents she was making. She unpacked them now, one by one.

First she lifted out the satin pincushion she'd made for Jessie, the seamstress. It was shaped like a strawberry and stuffed with a cup of sawdust from the butcher shop.

Next Samantha took out a book about a lost
dog. It was for Nathaniel, Jessie's baby. Samantha
had written it herself and stitched it together with
red yarn.

Grandmary's gift was underneath
the book. It was a heart made from
lace and stuffed with dried rose petals.
Samantha sniffed it. She knew Grandmary would
put it with her handkerchiefs to make them smell
pretty.

Mrs. Hawkins's gift was a chain to attach to her
glasses so she'd never lose them again. And for
Nellie, Samantha had made a blue velvet cape for
Lydia to wear. Samantha held the cape and thought
about how beautiful Lydia would look in it.

At last Samantha reached her favorite gift of
all. It was for Uncle Gard. Uncle Gard's present
wasn't finished yet, but already it was more
beautiful than anything Samantha had ever made.
It was a box—a small box, just the right size for cuff
links. Samantha had decorated it with pictures of
animals, leaves, berries, fruits, and flowers from her
collection of paper scraps. She had carefully cut out
each piece of scrap. Then she'd glued them, one by

one, to the sides of the box.

Now only the lid was left to be decorated. Samantha sat on the floor with her pot of glue and her collection of scraps spread around her. Very, very carefully she brushed the back of a purple pansy with glue and held it firmly on the box. After the glue had dried, she picked up one last picture—her favorite one. It was a heart with the words "with love" written on it. Carefully, Samantha placed it in the very center of the lid. It was perfect. She *knew* Uncle Gard would like this present best of any he would get on Christmas morning.

Just then someone knocked at her door.

"Miss Samantha."

"Just a minute, Jessie!" Samantha called. Quickly, she stuffed her presents back into the hatbox and pushed it under her bed.

"Open the door, child!"

Samantha hid her scrap collection next to the hatbox, scooted the chair out of her closet, and hurried to unlock her bedroom door.

"Come along, now. I've finished your Christmas dress. We just need to hem it," the seamstress said. Samantha followed her upstairs into the little sewing room. She could hardly wait to see the new party dress Jessie had made.

"Where is it?" Samantha asked, looking around the room.

"Oh, you'll see it in good time," Jessie said, smiling slyly. "Now, take off that dress, close your eyes, and raise your arms."

Samantha did as she was told and felt something crisp and cool slide over her head.

"Heavens!" Jessie gasped.

"What's the matter?" Samantha asked, keeping her eyes closed.

"Why, you've grown two inches since I measured you. Miss Samantha, you shoot up faster than smoke in a chimney!"

"May I open my eyes now, Jessie?"

"Not just yet. First let me fix the hem. That'll make a big difference."

Samantha waited patiently with her eyes still closed. "Jessie?"

"Mmmmm?" Jessie's mouth was full of pins.

"Ida Dean is having a Christmas party in two weeks. Do you think I can wear this dress?"

Jessie pulled the last pins out of her mouth. "I don't know, child. You'll have to ask your grandmother."

"Jessie . . . ?" Samantha started up again.

"Yes, Miss Samantha?"

"I just love Christmas. I love everything about it. Even getting ready for Christmas is fun."

"I'm sure it is," Jessie laughed.

"I've made all the decorations for the house already," Samantha added. "I've got paper snowflakes and cotton snowmen and things for the tree. And on Saturday morning, Nellie is coming over to help me make pinecone wreaths."

"Did you make the angels out of that blue silk I gave you?" Jessie asked.

"I made ten of them, just the way you showed me!"

"You *have* been working hard!" Jessie said.

"Now can I see myself, Jessie?" Samantha asked eagerly.

"Yes, it's all done."

Samantha opened her eyes and faced the long mirror. Slowly, she turned herself around. The red taffeta dress shimmered and made ever-so-soft

*The red taffeta dress shimmered and made
ever-so-soft swishing sounds as Samantha moved.*

swishing sounds as Samantha moved. It was the color of ripe cranberries. A snowy white lace collar circled the neck, and a crisp white sash wrapped her hips and tied in a bow in front.

"Oh, Jessie, this is the most gorgeous dress in the whole world," Samantha pronounced solemnly.

"I agree with you there, Miss Samantha! It's a dress fine enough for a princess, if I do say so myself!"

Samantha heard someone sniff. Elsa, the maid, was standing at the door scowling. "Playing dress-up at this hour!" she snipped. "It's all very well to fuss with them frills, but not at teatime. Your grandmother told me to fetch you, and here you are not even properly dressed!"

"Now, Elsa, Miss Samantha will be right down," Jessie answered.

"Fussing with frills at teatime!" Elsa muttered to herself as she turned. Her shoes scolded *tsk tsk tsk* as she walked down the hall.

Jessie helped Samantha out of the new dress and back into her regular clothes. Samantha straightened her stockings and raced downstairs.

"Grandmary, Grandmary!" she burst out.

She remembered to make a curtsy. "I have the most exciting news!"

"How delightful," replied her silver-haired grandmother as she lifted the teapot. "Come, let's have our tea."

Just as Samantha was sure she couldn't wait a moment longer, her grandmother asked, "And what is your news, Samantha?"

"My friend Ida Dean is having a Christmas party. It's a week from Thursday, and it's at night! Her brother will do magic tricks and we're going to play games, and it will be the most wonderful party of all. May I go? And may I wear my new Christmas dress?"

Grandmary took a sip of tea. "Samantha dear, you really must learn to ask only *one* question at a time. *Two* questions at once are quite . . . unbalancing. Now, as to the first question—of course you may go, my dear. And as to the second question—yes, you may wear your new dress. You grow so fast, you might as well get all the wear you can out of it."

"Thank you, Grandmary," Samantha said happily. "I'll have the best time."

"And now I have a surprise for you," Grandmary announced.

There was a long pause as Grandmary buttered
a biscuit. She was not one to hurry surprises.
Finally she said, "As you know, Samantha, your
Uncle Gardner will spend Christmas with us as he
always has. But this year he is not coming alone.
He is bringing Miss Cornelia Pitt with
him. She will celebrate the holidays
here in Mount Bedford and stay on
until the New Year."

Miss Cornelia Pitt? Grandmary
meant Cornelia! Samantha thought of
Uncle Gard's ginger-haired friend, who lived in
New York. Cornelia was beautiful and so elegant.
Her clothes were the latest style, and she always
smelled of violets.

"Remember, Samantha," Grandmary continued,
"Cornelia is a special friend of your uncle's. We
must make her feel welcome."

"Oh, I'll welcome her," Samantha said. "And
I'll make this the best Christmas *she's* ever had,
too. That will be easy. I've already made all the
decorations and planned the gingerbread house."

"That's very good of you, Samantha," Grandmary said. "But perhaps you have done enough already. Everyone in the house will be very busy now, and it may be best if you just stay out of the way."

Samantha wondered why grownups always thought the most helpful thing she could do was nothing at all. Didn't they understand what still had to be done? Someone had to string cranberries and hang snowflakes on the windows. Someone had to pick out just the right candy for the gingerbread house. Someone had to help Uncle Gard find a perfect Christmas tree. Samantha could do all those things. And now that Cornelia was coming, she had more to do. She would have to get one more present—something very nice and very elegant for Cornelia. But what? What??

"It's so *hard* to figure out gifts!" Samantha found herself saying aloud.

"What is that you said, dear?" Grandmary asked.

"I was just thinking, Grandmary, how hard it is to know what somebody might want for Christmas. I mean, most of the time you just have to guess!"

Grandmary smiled. "You're entirely correct, Samantha. Of course, sometimes a person might let you know what may be appropriate."

"Yes, Grandmary," Samantha said, remembering her own secret wish for Christmas. She thought of what Ida had said, and the words floated back to her. *You should ask her anyway,* they whispered. *The worst she can say is no.*

"Grandmary," Samantha said, clearing her throat.

"Yes, Samantha?" her grandmother answered, not looking up as she poured more tea.

"Grandmary, I wanted to ask if . . . if . . ."

"Yes?" Now Grandmary seemed to stare right through Samantha.

"Grandmary, I just wanted to ask you if . . . well . . ."

"Samantha dear, speak up. I can hardly hear you when you mumble!"

"Grandmary, I wanted to tell you that . . ."

"Come to the point, Samantha."

". . . that I think it's going to snow through the weekend!" Samantha blurted out, red-faced and shy.

"Yes, dear, I quite agree with you."

It was no use. Samantha knew she couldn't ask Grandmary for the doll. She didn't have the courage.

CHAPTER

THREE

—

DECORATIONS
AND
DISAPPOINTMENTS

 On Saturday morning, when their
pinecone wreaths were made, Samantha
showed Nellie some of the presents in
her pink hatbox. She saved Uncle Gard's box until
last. "And this is the best present of all," she said
proudly as she handed it to Nellie.

"Oh, it really is," Nellie agreed. "I know your
uncle will like it."

"He'll *love* it," Samantha insisted. "He'll know
it's the nicest thing I've ever made for anyone."

"What are you giving your grandmother?"
Nellie asked.

Samantha showed her the sweet-smelling
sachet she had made. "Grandmary says homemade

gifts are the best ones because you give of yourself when you make them. But I'll have to buy
Cornelia's present. There's not enough time to make
something really special for her," Samantha said.
"I wish I knew what to get."

"What about bath salts?" Nellie suggested.
"Mrs. Van Sicklen has some in a tall bottle with a
fancy glass top."

"Yes, bath salts are nice," Samantha agreed.
Then she shook her head. "But I don't think bath
salts are nice enough for Cornelia."

"How about hankies?" Nellie asked.

"Well, maybe if they had lace edges,"
Samantha said hopefully. Then she thought of
Cornelia riding in Uncle Gard's automobile, and
even hankies with lace edges seemed like a dull
sort of present. "No, Nellie, I need to think of
something *really* special."

"Perfume?" Nellie suggested.

"That would be special enough, but
I don't think I have enough money for
perfume." Samantha sighed. "Well, I can
go talk to Jessie later. Maybe she'll know what I
should get for Cornelia."

"I'm giving Mrs. Van Sicklen my biggest pinecone wreath," Nellie said. She looked proudly
at the wreaths she'd lined up on the floor of
Samantha's room. "Do you think she'll like it?"

"Of course she will," Samantha assured her
friend. "Everyone loves Christmas decorations."
She reached under her bed, pulled out a cardboard
box with DECORATIONS written on all four sides,
and took out the cotton snowmen, silk angels,
and paper snowflakes she'd been making since
Thanksgiving. "Look what I'm putting up this
afternoon," she said.

"Samantha, your house is going to look like
a fairyland," Nellie exclaimed.

"Especially with these snowflakes," Samantha
agreed.

Later that afternoon, after Nellie had gone
home, Samantha lugged her decoration box down
the long, winding staircase. *I'll trim the banister first,*

she thought. At the bottom of the stairs, she unpacked a long string of cranberries. She was about to wind it around the polished railing when a strange voice stopped her.

"Excuse me, young lady," said a tall, red-haired man. He wore a navy blue uniform almost like a soldier's. The words *Farrola Florist* were on the right pocket.

The man set down a large box that held spicy-scented garlands with enormous red bows. He drew a garland out slowly, handling it as delicately as if it were a snake. "Now if you would just step out of the way, miss," he continued as he began to wrap the garland gracefully around the banister.

"I have some decorations, too," Samantha told the man. "I have a cranberry garland. Well, I guess you'd call it a string of cranberries. It would look quite nice together with—"

"Please, miss," the red-haired man sighed, "if you could just stand back and try not to disturb the garland. It's a bit fragile."

Samantha stepped back and found herself standing on Hawkins's toes.

140

"Oh, Hawkins, I'm so sorry," she said.

"That's quite all right, Miss Samantha. Now, if you'll excuse me . . ."

Hawkins was carrying another box marked *Farrola Florist* into the parlor. Two more large boxes were already on the rug.

"What's in all these boxes?" asked Samantha.

"Holiday adornments," he said. "Christmas decorations." Samantha saw holly and laurel wreaths and bouquets of Christmas roses—red ones, of course. She counted four ropes of ivy, eight hoops of mistletoe, and two miniature trees. One was trimmed with little crab apples and one was full of tiny oranges. "Your grandmother wishes the house to be in full Yuletide splendor for Miss Cornelia's visit," Hawkins explained. He turned to drape an ivy rope across the fireplace mantel.

Samantha could not believe what she was seeing. "But Hawkins, I've already *made* decorations, lots of them, enough for the whole house!"

Hawkins was struggling so hard with the ivy that he didn't seem to hear.

Samantha picked up her box of decorations and walked into the dining room. No one was around, so she took out her fuzzy snowmen first. She hung six of them from the wall lamps, using green ribbon. Two more were soon propped up beside the huge meat platter on the china cabinet. Four snowmen stood together around a pile of pine-cones in the center of the table.

Using the tiniest drops of glue, Samantha stuck paper snowflakes to the dining room windows. She took down a small oil painting and in its place hung her largest pinecone wreath. The cranberry garland went across the dining room curtains.

When Samantha had finished, she sat down to admire her work. The whole room was like a tiny indoor forest filled with pinecones and red berries. Cotton snowmen peeked out from the dark furniture as if they were hiding behind tall trees. Paper snowflakes seemed to float on the windows. *It's beautiful,* Samantha thought. *It's like a winter wonderland—and I did it all by myself.*

Someone gasped. "Sakes alive! What is this nonsense?"

It was Elsa.

The maid went straight to the windows and began tearing off Samantha's snowflakes. "It's not as if a body didn't have enough to do, what with the washing and dusting and polishing," Elsa muttered. "And now having to put up with all this holiday hoopla. Whatever made the child set all them dustcatchers around?"

Samantha jumped out of her chair. "They're not dustcatchers! They're snowflakes and cranberry garlands and snowmen and . . . and . . . and I made them!"

Elsa was speechless for a moment. Then she

*"They're not dustcatchers! They're snowflakes
and I made them!" Samantha said.*

said firmly, "Mr. Hawkins and a young florist gentleman are decorating the house just as your grandmother wished—fine and fancy for Miss Cornelia's visit. So it's no use trying to tell me about your snowmice!"

"Snow*men*," Samantha sniffed, scooping up the decorations that Elsa had piled on the floor.

"Whatever," Elsa said. "Run along now. I've got the devil's own work dusting this chandelier. Miss Cornelia will be here for Christmas dinner, and it's got to sparkle."

"You'd think it was Cornelia Day, not Christmas Day," Samantha grumbled, almost loud enough for Elsa to hear. She went to the kitchen. Maybe a visit with Mrs. Hawkins would cheer her up.

The kitchen was perfumed with delicious smells. Two mince pies and a pound cake had just come out of the oven. There were homemade peppermint drops cooling on the table. At the sink, Mrs. Hawkins was pouring quince jam into glass jars. Her face was as red as the cranberry sauce that bubbled on the stove.

Samantha sat down at the table and popped one of the peppermint drops into her mouth. "You know, Mrs. Hawkins," she said, "I just thought of a good idea."

There was no answer.

"Mrs. Hawkins?"

"Yes, dear," Mrs. Hawkins replied, not looking up from her jam.

"I said that I just thought of something."

"Hmmm, what's that?"

"Well, we could cover the walls of the gingerbread house with peppermint drops and it would look like a magic candy house—like the candy house in *Hansel and Gretel*."

"Samantha," Mrs. Hawkins said with a sigh, "I know you'll be disappointed, but I don't see that we can make a gingerbread house after all. With your Uncle Gard's friend coming and your grandmother wanting everything so special for her, there's a tremendous lot of cooking to be done. There's just no time for a gingerbread house this year."

"Not *any* gingerbread house?" Samantha asked with disbelief. "Not even a little one?"

"Not even a little one, Samantha. Truly I'm

sorry, but I think you're old enough to understand."

"Yes, I understand," said Samantha sadly. "I really do, Mrs. Hawkins." She left the kitchen mumbling, "I understand that if Cornelia weren't coming, everything would be fine."

She picked up her box of decorations and hauled it up the stairway. The corner of the box bumped the garland on the banister and knocked a bow crooked. Samantha didn't straighten it.

In her room, Samantha unpacked her decorations again. *I'll put them up here,* she said to herself. *If everyone else thinks snowflakes are a bother, then they can stay out of my room.* She noticed that two of her best snowflakes had been ruined and decided to make new ones. She went to her desk to hunt for a pair of scissors.

Why is everyone making such a fuss over Cornelia? Samantha asked herself as she folded a piece of tissue paper. *There's nothing special about her. Nothing special at all. I don't know why I even bothered to worry about her present. I'll just give her hankies for Christmas. Plain, boring, lie-in-the-box hankies!*

There was a knock at Samantha's door. She

opened it to find Grandmary standing there.

"Samantha dear, your Uncle Gardner has just telephoned to say that he and Cornelia will arrive late Thursday afternoon. We must welcome Cornelia properly, so I am afraid that going to a party that evening is out of the question. You will need to send Ida Dean your regrets."

"Oh, Grandmary, no!" Samantha cried.

Grandmary's face said it was useless to argue, and just to be sure she added, "It is the polite thing to do, Samantha." She said it kindly, but Samantha knew she didn't expect to say it again.

Stupid Cornelia is ruining Christmas, Samantha thought. *She's ruining it for everybody, but mostly she's ruining it for me. I'm not allowed to decorate my house and I can't make a gingerbread house, either. Now I can't go to Ida's party, so I won't be able to play charades or see magic tricks or wear my beautiful new dress!*

"I hate Cornelia!" Samantha said when she was sure Grandmary couldn't hear her. Slowly, hot tears began to roll down her cheeks.

"I'm glad I don't have enough money to buy her perfume. I won't buy her handkerchiefs, either.

I wouldn't give Cornelia bath salts in a paper bag. In fact, I won't give her anything at all for Christmas." The tears came faster, and Samantha began to sob.

SOMEONE
VERY SPECIAL

"Your house looks especially lovely
with all the Christmas decorations,"
Cornelia said. Sunlight poured through
the parlor windows and danced in her soft, wavy
hair.

"Thank you," Grandmary answered. "We did
want things to be festive for you."

Samantha didn't say anything. She didn't even
look at Cornelia.

"I hope the trip down wasn't too tiring for
you," said Grandmary as she passed a plate of tiny
tea sandwiches.

"Oh, no," Cornelia replied. "I do love motorcars,
and Gard—I mean Gardner—is such a good driver."

Grandmary smiled. "You are certainly brave, my dear, to ride in those new machines."

"I love travel of any kind," Cornelia responded, her brown eyes sparkling. "When the new flying machines begin to carry passengers, I plan to ride in one of them, too."

So do I! Samantha thought. *I'd love to see Mount Bedford the way a bird sees it!*

Grandmary raised her eyebrows. "Well," she said to Cornelia, "I don't think there will ever be much chance of ladies traveling in airplanes!"

"I'm not so sure," Cornelia said gently, surprising Samantha with how gracefully she could disagree with Grandmary. "I've read in the newspaper that travel by airplane might be possible one day, even across the ocean."

Samantha looked at Grandmary. She knew Grandmary thought this was nonsense. But her grandmother merely replied, "Perhaps."

Uncle Gard laughed. "By Jupiter, any sort of travel is fine with me! Let them put me in a hot air balloon or in a rickshaw or on an elephant. I'd even let them shoot me out of a cannon!"

"Gardner!" Grandmary exclaimed. She

pretended to be shocked, and Samantha giggled.

"Of course I think the *best* form of travel is sledding," Uncle Gard added. He turned to Samantha. "Don't you, Sam?"

"Oh, yes," Samantha agreed, "only I haven't gone yet this winter."

"Well, why don't we go sledding tomorrow morning?" suggested Cornelia.

"Do you really think . . . ?" Grandmary began.

Cornelia's large brown eyes were soft and earnest. "It's such good, wholesome exercise," she said.

"Please, Grandmary," Samantha pleaded. "I *love* sledding!"

"All right." Grandmary smiled. "Sledding tomorrow morning will be fine."

"Hurrah!" cried Samantha. Right then she made up her mind to give Cornelia something nice for Christmas after all. Maybe bath salts. The kind in the tall bottle with the fancy glass top.

The sun sparkled on Fairwind Hill the next morning. The sky was deep blue and cloudless, the air was clean and cool, and all of Mount Bedford lay below, tucked under a soft, thick blanket of snow.

"I love this hill," Uncle Gard said as they pulled the sled to the top. "When I was a boy, I'd come up here to imagine I was in heaven."

Cornelia smiled. "Gard, I think you could imagine *anything* if you tried."

"I couldn't imagine life without you," Gard murmured.

Samantha caught his words. *Uncle Gard is in love!* she said to herself. *He loves Cornelia!*

"Sam," Uncle Gard called over his shoulder, "who's going to steer?"

"You steer the sled, Uncle Gard. I want to be in the middle."

"All right," Uncle Gard laughed. "Let's go!"

The three piled on the sled. Uncle Gard sat in front, then Samantha, and behind them both, Cornelia.

"I feel somewhat like a caboose," Cornelia said, making Samantha laugh.

"Hold on!" Uncle Gard called. With a tremendous whoosh they were gone, skimming down the hillside at top speed.

"Ooooh!" cried Samantha with delight.

"Hurrah for us!" came Cornelia's unladylike shout.

The sled slid faster and faster, skidding and hopping down the hill. "Watch out!" Uncle Gard yelled.

But it was too late.

The sled veered out of control, narrowly missed a tree, and tipped over. The passengers spilled out into the snow.

"Oof!" Samantha grunted, wiping the soft powder from her face.

Uncle Gard was in front of her, laughing and pointing back up the hill. Samantha turned to see what he thought was so funny. It was Cornelia! She had landed on her stomach, and her hat had flown right off her head. She looked most unladylike with her legs tangled, her face red as a beet, and her beautiful hair all stringy and wet. But she was laughing, too! Samantha had never seen anything like it—a grown-up lady who knew how to play.

*Samantha turned to see what he thought
was so funny. It was Cornelia!*

Cornelia is fun! I see why Uncle Gard loves her, Samantha thought.

"Come on!" Cornelia cried, pulling herself up and dusting off the snow. "Let's do it again!"

And they did. They sledded until they were so out of breath, their clothes so wet, and their noses so red that they could do nothing but hurry home to a hot lunch with Grandmary. After lunch they decided to go shopping. They piled into Uncle Gard's automobile, and with a loud *ooh-wah ooh-wah* from the horn, they rumbled off toward High Street.

This year the stores seemed more beautiful than ever. Miss Smith's Stationery Shop had a revolving Christmas tree made of Christmas cards. As a music box played "Joy to the World," the tree turned round and round.

Mr. Jerome, the shoemaker, had four mechanical elves in his window. They hammered, stitched, and polished tiny shoes. Their mouths opened and closed as they worked, and their pointy-hatted heads turned from side to side.

"Aren't they cute?" Samantha asked.

She had seen the elves every Christmas she could remember, yet each year they delighted her as if she had never seen them before.

"Yes, I love the store windows at Christmas-time, too," Cornelia replied.

Next they came to Mr. Carruthers's Candy Shop. Samantha thought Mr. Carruthers's shop was always a wonderful place, but now she thought it was spectacular. Large red bins shaped like sleighs were heaped with sweets.

"Oh, don't those look delicious?" Cornelia pointed to the mounds of light and dark chocolates on a small silver tray inside a glass case. "I just love chocolate truffles," she said.

"Well, these are the finest in Mount Bedford," Mr. Carruthers informed her. "Jolie Chocolates. They arrived just this week from France."

"They do look special," Uncle Gard remarked, "although I prefer jelly beans myself."

Samantha had paused in front of some colored sugar wafers. "Oh, Samantha, wouldn't these be perfect on a gingerbread house?" Cornelia asked her. "When I was a girl, I always decorated a gingerbread house."

"I always decorated a gingerbread house, too," Samantha said. "This year Mrs. Hawkins doesn't have time to help me, though."

"Then why don't you and I make a gingerbread house?" Cornelia asked. "We could do it tomorrow morning."

"Oh, I'd like that. I'd like that very much!" Samantha said. They picked out all the trimmings right then. Mr. Carruthers filled several paper bags with lemon drops, sugar wafers, jelly beans, and honey sticks.

Cornelia is really too nice for bath salts, Samantha thought as they walked out of the store. *She deserves something special. Maybe I'll get her handkerchiefs. Linen handkerchiefs with lace edges.*

When they crossed Felter Street, Samantha heard the tinkly music of toy pianos. "Let's go to Schofield's Toy Store!" she cried.

The store was crowded, but Uncle Gard, Cornelia, and Samantha managed to make their way inside. Uncle Gard led Cornelia to the back of the shop to look at the toy soldiers, and Samantha went straight to the window to look at the dolls.

When she saw that the lovely Nutcracker doll was still there, her heart sank. She'd hoped it would be gone because Grandmary had bought it for her, but she knew that was a foolish hope. Grandmary didn't even know that Samantha wanted this doll more than anything in the world. Grandmary *couldn't* know that because Samantha hadn't told her. And now Samantha was sure that someone else would buy the doll for some other girl—maybe for one of the girls in the store right this minute.

Just then a hand reached into the display and picked up the beautiful Nutcracker doll. "Oh, look at this doll! Isn't she exquisite?"

Samantha was startled. She hadn't heard anyone come up behind her. She turned to find Cornelia.

"And look at the tiny Nutcracker in her arms," Cornelia exclaimed. "This is the most wonderful doll in the store. Don't you think so, Samantha?"

"Oh, yes," Samantha agreed out loud. To herself she said, *Cornelia understands. She knows what's special.* And for just a moment, she forgot to be sad about the doll she would never have.

Just then Uncle Gard returned. "The toy

soldiers said we'd better march. Grandmary will worry if we're late."

They pushed their way out of the busy store, but when they reached the car, Samantha announced, "I won't be coming home with you."

"What do you mean?" Uncle Gard asked.

"I—I forgot something. I forgot to—to buy the vanilla Mrs. Hawkins asked me to pick up for her," Samantha lied. "I'll get it and walk home."

"Nonsense, Sam," Uncle Gard said. "We'll go together."

"No—no, really," Samantha said, "I would rather go alone and walk. I love the streets at Christmastime."

Uncle Gard was about to say no again, but something in Samantha's voice must have told him this was important. After a pause he said, "All right, Sam, go if you want. But don't be late!"

When she was sure the automobile had turned the corner, Samantha ran back up High Street to Mr. Carruthers's Candy Shop. The little bell over the door tinkled as she went inside. "Well, young lady," Mr. Carruthers said, "how can I help you this time?"

"A pound of Jolie French chocolates, please."

"A whole pound?" Mr. Carruthers asked, his white eyebrows twitching up with surprise.

"A whole pound," Samantha repeated.

"This must be for someone really special, Samantha."

"Oh, yes, Mr. Carruthers—someone *very* special."

EXCHANGING GIFTS

On Christmas Eve morning, Samantha and Cornelia put the finishing touches on their gingerbread house. Their hands were sticky with icing and Samantha's cheek was striped with chocolate, but their gingerbread cottage was neat and tidy. It wasn't as large as the house Samantha had planned, and it didn't have a drawbridge, but there was a path of colored sugar wafers that looked like cobblestones leading up to the front door.

"You're clever in the kitchen, Miss Cornelia," Mrs. Hawkins said.

Cornelia blushed and pushed a silky curl out of her eyes. "Oh, it's nothing really," she answered.

"I've always enjoyed cooking, Mrs. Hawkins."

"Well, it's a credit to you," Mrs. Hawkins declared solemnly. "Many a lady nowadays wouldn't know batter from butter!"

"Did I hear someone say 'butter'?" Uncle Gard asked, coming into the kitchen. "Good grief, Mrs. Hawkins! I do hope you're not buttering up Cornelia. We wouldn't want her to slip away!"

Samantha groaned. "Uncle Gard, that's an awful joke."

"Is it?" Uncle Gard asked innocently. "Well, I suppose it's an awful *good* joke."

"Oh, Uncle Gard, please stop," Samantha said.

"Okay, Sam. But it's time to go if we want to find our Christmas tree. Hawkins has already harnessed the horses."

"I'll be ready before you can say 'Merry Christmas'!" Samantha called, racing to get her mittens, hat, and coat.

Hawkins held the horses steady as Samantha and Uncle Gard climbed into the sleigh. Uncle Gard slapped the reins hard over the horses' backs, and the sleigh glided down the path to the street. For several minutes Samantha and her uncle rode in silence. They shared the red wool blanket and waved to passing neighbors. Then, almost to herself, Samantha said, "Tomorrow is Christmas."

"It's come pretty quickly, hasn't it, Sam?"

"No, I don't think so," Samantha replied. "I've been planning for months. And of course," she added with a mischievous smile, "it took a long time to get *your* present ready."

"Oh?" Uncle Gard asked, pretending not to be interested.

"Yes. It's the nicest present of all, and you'll

never, never guess what it is," Samantha said.

"Of course I will!" Uncle Gard announced. "Let me try. Is it smaller than a breadbox?"

"Quite a bit, yes."

"Is it green?"

"Parts of it are," Samantha told him.

"Could I ride on it?"

"Not at all," Samantha giggled.

"Does it sing?"

"No."

"Can it do handsprings?"

Samantha laughed. "No! Guess some more."

"Is it something that closes up?"

"It could . . ." Samantha said cautiously.

"Could I wear it on my head in summer?"

"You'd look silly if you did!"

"Aha! I know what it is!" Uncle Gard declared.

"Tell me," Samantha said.

"It's a baby turtle, of course."

"A baby turtle?" Samantha gasped. "How do you figure that, Uncle Gard?"

"Because, Sam, everyone knows a baby turtle is smaller than a breadbox, cannot sing or do handsprings, is part green, can close up, cannot be

165

ridden, and would look silly on my head in summer."

"Well, you're wrong," Samantha said. "It's not a baby turtle. It's something I made. And it's very beautiful. In fact, it is the most beautiful thing I've ever made for anyone."

"I'm sure I will love it, Sam," Uncle Gard said.

"I wonder what you'll give *me* for Christmas?" Samantha asked slyly.

"No, you don't!" Uncle Gard said. "Don't you try to trick me into telling you."

"Just give me some clues. Please, Uncle Gard," Samantha begged.

"Okay, I'll give you three clues and no more. Clue number one: like a good schoolgirl, it uses *notes*. Clue number two: unlike Samantha, it always *plays* alone. Clue number three: it's *bound* to please you."

Samantha was so puzzled by these clues that she sat deep in thought while the sleigh glided through the silent woods. When they reached the frozen river, Uncle Gard stopped the horses and tied the reins to a low willow branch. He lifted an ax from the back of the sleigh and caught

166

Samantha's hand as she jumped down into the soft
snow. Then they walked together, looking for just
the right tree.

"This is it, Uncle Gard," Samantha said at last.

"You're right, Samantha. It's a real beauty."

Uncle Gard chopped away. The ax's loud
whacks echoed through the stillness, and Samantha
didn't talk as they dragged the tree back to the
sleigh. On the way home, the horses' bells jingled
brightly to the *clip-clop* rhythm of their hooves.

"I believe Mrs. Hawkins really outdid herself
this year," Uncle Gard said as he pushed his chair
back from the table. "Dinner was a feast!"

The aroma of plum pudding still hung in the
air. Red candles burned low in their polished
holders. And Samantha couldn't wait a moment
longer. "Grandmary, now may we decorate the
tree?" she asked.

"Of course," Grandmary replied.

They gathered in the parlor and began to

unpack the ornaments. Grandmary lifted a pair of
little glass slippers out of the big oak chest. "These
belong where they'll catch the light," she said. "I've
watched them sparkle since I was six
years old." She draped their golden
cord over a long branch. Uncle Gard
put a brass trumpet nearby. Cornelia
placed the long-necked crystal swans near the top
of the tree, where they seemed to float in the
branches. And Samantha hung all of her blue silk
angels right in the front, where Cornelia insisted
they should be.

Soon it was time to attach the little white
candles. Then slowly, one by one, Uncle Gard lit
them. The effect was glorious. China rosebuds
gleamed, crystal swans sparkled, and silk angels
shone in the flickering light. Foil-wrapped sugar-
plums bobbed and twinkled, and miniature brass
trumpets winked brightly. Grandmary's glass
slippers seemed to dance.

They watched in silence, until Cornelia stepped
over to the piano and began to play and sing:
"O Christmas tree, O Christmas tree,
How lovely are your branches."

Uncle Gard joined in, and Samantha and Grandmary sang, too. When the song was finished, Cornelia began another Christmas carol. They all sang and sang until the last candles on their beautiful tree burned low.

Later that night, while Samantha lay awake listening to street carolers in the distance, she thought again of the lovely Nutcracker doll. *Right now she's probably under some girl's Christmas tree, wrapped in pretty paper and waiting to be opened,* Samantha thought. She tried to think of something else, but it was no use. *If only I had even asked*

169

Grandmary for the doll, at least I'd have a chance of finding it under my tree tomorrow morning, Samantha thought. *Now there's no chance at all. None.* She fell asleep to the sound of Christmas carols and dreamed of the beautiful doll dancing away from her, farther and farther away.

"Where is everybody?" Samantha asked on Christmas morning. She had hurried downstairs with her pink hatbox full of gifts to find that she was the only one awake. The grandfather clock in the parlor chimed seven o'clock.

Samantha looked around the parlor. The Christmas stockings at the mantel bulged with treats. A small mountain of presents already stood underneath the tree. "To Dear Samantha from Grandmary" was written on a box that wasn't nearly as big as the doll in Schofield's window. Samantha sighed and began to arrange her own presents under the tree.

She heard a rustling sound behind her. "Merry

Christmas, Samantha," Cornelia said. She wore a forest green dress and carried a pile of presents.

"Merry Christmas," Samantha answered.

A moment later, Grandmary and Uncle Gard were in the parlor, too. "Merry Christmas!" Samantha called.

Grandmary sat down next to the tree. "I've asked Mrs. Hawkins to hold breakfast until eight, so we can exchange gifts right away. I know how you hate to wait, Samantha." She handed Samantha a package. "For you, my dear. Merry Christmas."

Inside was a sewing kit, a very grown-up one with forty different colored threads, a thick package of needles, and a cat-shaped pincushion. Samantha loved the way everything in the kit was arranged in its own special compartment.

"Oh, Grandmary, thank you," exclaimed Samantha. "Thank you so much." She gave her grandmother a warm hug. "Now I have a present for you," she said. She handed Grandmary her gift.

"It has a delightful fragrance," Grandmary said. "I can smell it right through the paper!"

"Can you guess what it is, Grandmary?"

"Not at all, dear. I'm quite perplexed so far."

Very slowly Grandmary took off the paper. When she found the heart-shaped sachet she said, "Samantha, you're a dear and clever girl. This is very lovely."

Next came a present from Uncle Gard to Samantha. "Here's your answer to those riddles, Sam," he said.

Samantha ripped off the wrapping paper and found a red leather book of Christmas carols. She turned the pages carefully, humming songs as she went. When she reached the end of the book, Samantha found a golden key. She wound it and a music box began to play her favorite song of all—"O Christmas Tree."

"Now I understand, Uncle Gard!" Samantha exclaimed. "You said my present would use notes and play alone because it's a music box. And it *is* bound to please me because it's a book of my favorite Christmas carols, too. Now I can listen to them all year round. Thank you."

Samantha was about to give Uncle Gard a small square box covered in blue tissue paper, but

Cornelia handed her a large package instead.

"Go ahead, open yours first, Sam," Uncle Gard said with a wink.

Samantha had never seen anything wrapped so elegantly. She untied the silk ribbon and carefully rolled it up. "Cornelia, is this from New York?" asked Samantha.

"Open it and see."

Samantha smoothed away the silvery wrapping paper and slowly lifted the lid from the box. "Cornelia!" she gasped. "It's the Nutcracker doll! Oh, I've wanted this doll for the longest time. How did you ever know?"

"I didn't know, Samantha," Cornelia said. "Truly I didn't. It's only that *I* liked the doll so much, I thought perhaps you might, too."

"I do," Samantha said. She hugged the doll as if she'd never let it go. "I love her. I love her more than any other doll in the whole world. Thank you, Cornelia. Thank you so much!"

With the doll still in her arms, Samantha reached under the tree. Once again she picked up the small square box wrapped in blue tissue paper.

*Samantha hugged the doll
as if she'd never let it go.*

But this time she turned to Cornelia and handed it to her. "Merry Christmas, Cornelia," Samantha whispered, suddenly shy.

"And Merry Christmas, Uncle Gard," Samantha said more loudly, handing him a larger package tied with a big pink bow.

Uncle Gard got his present unwrapped first. "By Jove, Sam!" he said when he opened the candy. "There must be a pound of chocolates here. You do spoil me!"

"Oh, Samantha, it's so very pretty!" Cornelia exclaimed when she saw the decorated box. "Why, look at all these tiny pictures! This must have taken you a long time to make."

"It did," Samantha said honestly. "That box took me longer than any other thing I've made. Ever!"

"I will keep my jewelry in it and treasure it always," Cornelia said.

Samantha caught Uncle Gard's happy wink. She thought he guessed that the box had been made for cuff links, but he seemed to understand why she'd given it to Cornelia.

Now Uncle Gard turned to Cornelia and said,

"I think you need something special to keep in such a beautiful box, my dear." He handed her a tiny gift wrapped in dark red paper with a large gold bow on top. When Cornelia opened it, a diamond ring sparkled in the Christmas morning sunlight.

"Oh, Gard," she murmured softly.

But Samantha was so overjoyed she shouted, "It's an engagement ring! They're going to marry! Grandmary, isn't it wonderful?"

"Children, I'm so happy." Grandmary's voice was quivery, and she had to dab her eyes with her hankie.

"When is the wedding?" Samantha couldn't wait to find out.

"In the spring," the couple answered together.

"You *will* be my bridesmaid, won't you, Samantha?" Cornelia asked.

"Yes, I'd love to!" Samantha answered, and gave her a big hug. "Oh, Cornelia, this *has* been the best Christmas ever!"

TO CHRISTOPHER WALLACE DRAPER

HAPPY BIRTHDAY,
Samantha!

BY VALERIE TRIPP

CHAPTER
ONE
—

PETTICOATS AND
PETIT FOURS

 "SURPRISE!" shouted two excited
voices. "Happy birthday, Samantha!"

Samantha sat up and rubbed her
eyes. Two redheaded curlytops whirled into her
room, jumped up on her bed, and pushed a huge
bouquet of roses into her arms. "This is for you!"
said the redhead named Agnes.

"Jiminy!" exclaimed Samantha. "It's beautiful!"

"We made it ourselves," added Agatha proudly.
Agatha looked exactly like Agnes. They were Aunt
Cornelia's twin sisters. Now that Uncle Gard and
Cornelia were married, Agnes and Agatha were
Samantha's newest friends and favorite relatives.

Samantha put her nose deep into the roses.

"Thank you!" she said. "No one ever gave me flowers for my birthday before."

"I knew you'd like them," said Agnes happily. "It was my idea to give you a bouquet."

"Well, it was my idea to wrap the stems in lace," insisted Agatha.

Samantha looked at the bottom of the bouquet. "Where did you get all this nice lace?" she asked. "It looks sort of like it came off a petticoat."

The twins looked at each other and giggled.

"Did you cut up your petticoat?" Samantha asked.

"Not exactly," said Agatha. She leaned back and twisted one of her red curls around her finger. "There was already a rip where the ruffle was attached. We just sort of helped the rip get bigger until the ruffle fell off."

"Gosh!" said Samantha. "Grandmary would be furious if I cut up one of my petticoats. Won't your mother be angry?"

"Oh, no," said Agnes lightly. "That petticoat was getting too small for us anyway."

"Besides," said Agatha, "our mother is used to us and our ideas by now."

Samantha laughed out loud. Sometimes it
seemed to her that Agnes's and Agatha's ideas spilled
out all over the place, like popcorn popping out of
a pot. During the week of their visit, the twins had
turned Grandmary's quiet house in Mount Bedford
topsy-turvy. Samantha liked it that way.

Agnes sprawled on Samantha's bed, swinging
her legs over the side. "Hurry and get dressed," she
said. "We smelled something absolutely
scrumptious coming from the kitchen."

"Ooooh! I bet Mrs. Hawkins is
making a birthday treat for breakfast!"
said Samantha as she scrambled out
of bed. "I'll be dressed in a jiffy."
She pulled her long underwear out of the drawer.

"Oh, don't bother with that," said Agnes. "No
one wears long underwear anymore." Agnes and
Agatha were from New York City, so they knew all
about the latest fashions.

"I *have* to wear it," sighed Samantha. "It's one of
Grandmary's rules: long underwear from September
to the end of June." She pulled the itchy underwear
onto one leg.

"Jeepers!" exclaimed Agatha. "What an old-

"Then don't wear long underwear," said Agnes.
"Make up your own mind for once."

fashioned rule! You'll roast if you wear that today."

Samantha held out her leg and looked at the underwear. "I do hate it," she said.

"Then don't wear it," said Agnes simply. "Make up your own mind for once."

Samantha sat up very straight. "I'm ten years old today," she said. "I guess that's old enough to think for myself about things like underwear." She peeled off the underwear, rolled it up into a ball, and shoved it to the back of the dresser drawer. When she pulled her stockings on over her bare legs, she felt deliciously light and free.

"Come on," she said to the twins as she buttoned up her dress. "Let's go have breakfast." She grabbed her bouquet off the bed. "I can't wait to show these roses to Hawkins."

"Hawkins has already seen them," said Agatha as the girls trotted down the hall. "They're from his bush."

Samantha stopped still. "Uh-oh," she said. "No one is allowed to touch Hawkins's special rosebush. No one!"

"Don't worry," laughed Agnes. "There were millions of roses on that bush. Hawkins won't mind that we borrowed a few."

And to Samantha's surprise, Agnes was right. Hawkins didn't mind about the roses. "What a lovely birthday surprise!" he said. His eyes twinkled. "Mrs. Hawkins and I have a birthday surprise for you, too, Miss Samantha." He pushed open the kitchen door, and there was Mrs. Hawkins with a plate of blueberry muffins. One of the muffins had a candle stuck right in the middle.

"Oooh!" exclaimed Samantha. "Blueberry muffins!"

"Quick! Make a wish!" said Agatha. "Blow out the candle."

"That's easy," laughed Samantha. She scrunched her eyes shut and wished that being ten would be completely different from being nine. She was ready for some changes. Then she blew the candle out with one puff.

As the twins clapped, Mrs. Hawkins said, "Well, that *was* easy. But this afternoon, you'll have a cake with ten candles. You'll surely have to huff and puff then, love."

Agatha bounced on her chair. "I have a wonderful idea, Mrs. Hawkins!" she exclaimed.

"Instead of one cake with ten candles, you could make ten little cakes and put a candle on each one of them!"

"Ten cakes?" asked Mrs. Hawkins. She sounded doubtful.

"Ten little teeny-tiny cakes," said Agatha. "They're called petit fours. Ladies have them at all the fancy tea parties in New York."

"Petit fours," Samantha repeated. "They sound so elegant. Could you try to make them, Mrs. Hawkins? Please?"

"Well, I don't know," said Mrs. Hawkins slowly. "We never had anything so different before."

"That's why it's such a wonderful idea," pleaded Samantha. "No one in Mount Bedford has ever had ten cakes. All the girls will be so surprised."

Mrs. Hawkins smiled at Samantha. "If you want ten cakes, you shall have them, love," she said. "I guess I can try something new."

"I have an idea for something new, too," Agnes piped up. "What if you shaped each girl's ice cream in a little

187

ice cream mold? That's how they do it at the big ice cream parlors in the city."

Samantha was very excited. The twins had such good ideas! "Could we change the ice cream, too?" she asked Hawkins. "Except I still want it to be peppermint. That's my absolute favorite kind."

Hawkins laughed. "We can change the shape of the ice cream without changing the flavor," he said. "As soon as I've washed the ice cream freezer, you may help me make it."

"Meanwhile, you chickadees scoot outside," said Mrs. Hawkins, rolling up her sleeves. "I don't want you underfoot while I'm making your petit fours."

Samantha and the twins finished their blueberry muffins and hurried outside into the sunshine. The trees were covered with shiny green leaves, as if they'd decorated themselves in honor of Samantha's birthday. Samantha was telling the twins how ice cream was made when a voice behind them said, "Hey, carrot heads."

It was Eddie Ryland, Samantha's pesky next-door neighbor.

Agnes scowled at him. "Don't say 'hey,'" she said. "Hay is for horses."

"You ought to know," said Eddie. "You eat like a horse."

The girls rolled their eyes at each other while Eddie laughed at his own joke. "So, what are you ninnies doing today?" he went on.

"Nothing," said all three girls quickly.

But just at that moment, Hawkins appeared with the freezer.

"I know! You're making ice cream!" said Eddie. "I know *everything* about ice cream. I'll help."

"No!" said the girls in one voice.

"You just go away, Eddie," Agatha ordered.

"Who's going to make me?" Eddie challenged.

"*I'll* make you," Agatha began. Samantha saw that Agatha was making a fist. She knew Agatha would punch Eddie right in the nose if she wanted to. Not even Grandmary's strictest rule—GIRLS DON'T FIGHT—would stop Agatha once she was mad.

"Oh, all right, Eddie," Samantha said quickly. "You can help us make ice cream, but don't be a pest." She whispered to the twins, "Just ignore him. Maybe he'll go away."

The girls and Eddie watched as Hawkins

poured ice chips into the ice cream freezer. "Now it's time to add the salt," said Samantha. She scooped up handfuls of rock salt from a sack and poured the salt on the ice.

"Use just enough to keep the ice melted," warned Hawkins.

"And keep it away from the lid of the container," Eddie added in a know-it-all voice. "Because if any salt gets inside, the ice cream will be ruined."

"We don't need you to boss us, Eddie," said Agatha. She pushed her shoulder in front of

Eddie to block his view.

"This ice cream is going to be the best ice cream anyone ever ate," Samantha said happily as Hawkins began turning the crank of the freezer.

"I can't wait to taste it," said Agnes.

"Me, either," said Samantha.

"Me, either," said Agatha.

"Me, either," said Eddie. But the girls just ignored him.

THE PARTY

Samantha was tying a big bow in the sash of her pinafore when Grandmary came into her room. "Happy birthday, dear," she said. "I have something special for you to wear at your party. Turn and face the mirror."

Samantha was very still while Grandmary stood behind her and fastened an old-fashioned circlet of silk rosebuds in her hair. "Oh, Grandmary," Samantha sighed. "It's lovely."

Grandmary smiled. "Your mother wore this circlet at her tenth birthday party. I'm sure she would have been happy to see it passed on to you now. You look just as pretty as she did."

"Thank you very much," Samantha said.

"You are welcome, my dear," said Grandmary. "Now let's go down and wait for your guests. It's almost time for them to arrive."

Samantha felt fluttery with excitement as she stood in front of the house next to Grandmary. She couldn't wait until her friends saw the wonderful surprises she and the twins had planned for them. One by one the girls came up the walk, dressed in their very best party dresses. Each girl carried her favorite doll in one arm and a brightly wrapped present for Samantha in the other. Even though Samantha knew everyone well, she felt a little shy as her friends said hello and curtsied to her and to Grandmary. The guests were shy, too, especially when they saw Agnes and Agatha. The twins looked very grown-up in their blue party dresses, which were the latest style from New York.

The girls sat quietly in a circle of wicker chairs on the sunny side lawn. They sat up straight, their legs crossed at the ankles. Their dolls sat up straight, too, and stared at each other across the circle. Samantha tried to begin a polite, grown-up conversation. "Well," she said at last. "It certainly is a nice day."

The girls sat up straight, their legs crossed at the ankles.
Their dolls sat up straight, too.

"Yes!" everyone agreed. Then all the girls were quiet again. A breeze ruffled their big hairbows and the skirts of their dresses. It looked as if a flock of pale butterflies was fluttering rather nervously over the smooth green grass.

No one seemed to have anything to say, so Samantha tried again. "It is quite warm though—"

"Why don't you open your gifts?" Agnes interrupted.

"Good idea," murmured the rest of the girls. One by one they stepped forward and handed Samantha their presents. Everyone oohed and aahed politely as she opened a box of colored pencils from Ida, a fan from Ruth, and a big book of piano exercises from Edith Eddleton. Agnes and Agatha kept their present for last. They giggled as they came forward together and handed Samantha a big square box.

Samantha lifted the lid and held up a stout, cheerful-looking stuffed bear. Everyone squealed with delight. "A teddy bear!" exclaimed Samantha. "I love it!" She gave the bear a big hug.

"Teddy bears are the newest thing in New York," said Agnes, beaming. "We wanted you to have one of your very own."

"Thanks!" said Samantha.

"Oh, may I hold him?" asked Ida. "He's just so cute."

The friendly bear was passed from girl to girl. But after he had gone around the circle, the party got too quiet again. Everyone was trying so hard to be polite and grown-up, they were as stiff as the lace on their collars.

Samantha was relieved when a car came roaring up the drive with an ear-splitting *ooh-wah ooh-wah!* "Uncle Gard! Aunt Cornelia!" she exclaimed. Her guests bounced out of their chairs. "Hello! Hello!" they called as they followed Samantha over to the car.

Uncle Gard came straight to Samantha without even stopping to take off his driving goggles. He lifted her up into the air. "Happy samday, Bertha!" he said. All the girls giggled and Uncle Gard pretended to be confused. "Wait a minute. That's not right," he said. "I'll have to do that over." He lifted Samantha up again, gave her a kiss, and said, "Happy birthday, Samantha!"

"Oh, Gard!" laughed Aunt Cornelia. She leaned

over and gave Samantha a soft kiss. "Happy, happy birthday, Samantha," she said. "There's someone I'd like you to meet." Aunt Cornelia reached into the car and lifted out a little brown and white puppy. "This is Jip, the newest member of our family," she explained.

When Samantha took Jip in her arms, he reached up and licked her chin with his warm, rough tongue. "He's perfect," Samantha sighed.

"Put him down," said Agatha, "and I'll make him do his tricks."

"Remember to keep an eye on him," warned Cornelia as Samantha carried Jip over to the side lawn. "He's frisky and he likes to run."

Samantha put Jip on the grass inside the circle of chairs. "Sit, Jip," commanded Agatha. Jip wagged his tail, but he didn't sit. "He doesn't always do what you ask him to," Agatha admitted. "Sit, Jip!" she commanded again. But Jip ignored her. He began to run wildly around the circle of girls, barking at their feet.

"He likes shoes," explained Agnes. So all the girls sat in their chairs and danced their feet up and down in front of Jip. Jip ran from girl to girl, growling and jumping at their shoes and having a wonderful time. Then Agatha's foot knocked over a box, and the teddy bear tumbled out. To the girls' delight, Jip began to growl at the bear.

"Look at Jip!" laughed Agatha. "He's acting like a ferocious lion." She picked up the bear and waggled it in front of Jip's face. "Grr!" she growled. "Come and get me, Jip!"

Jip leaped up and yanked the bear out of Agatha's hands, then scampered across the lawn, dragging the bear by its leg. "Jip!" called Samantha. "Stop!"

"Let's go get him!" yelled Agatha. Agnes knocked over her chair in her hurry to get up. All the girls squealed with glee. They jumped out of their chairs and ran after Jip and the twins.

Jip led the girls to the back of the house, in dizzy circles around the oak tree, across the drive, through the lilac hedge, and into the Rylands' yard. Finally, they caught up with him next to the Rylands' birdbath.

"Grab him!" yelled Agatha. She started to take a running leap.

"No, stop!" said Samantha. "I've got a better

idea." She took off her shoe and dangled it in front of Jip. "Here, Jip," she called in a friendly voice.

Jip perked up his ears. "Come and get the shoe, Jip," Samantha said. And sure enough, Jip dropped the teddy bear, trotted over to Samantha, and grabbed the shoe in his mouth. Samantha quickly picked him up. His paws left muddy polka dots on her lacy pinafore.

"Hurray!" cheered the girls.

"But where's the bear?" asked Edith Eddleton.

"I have it," someone said in a bragging voice. And there was Eddie, holding Samantha's teddy bear by its nose.

"Eddie Ryland, you give me that teddy bear," ordered Samantha.

"No!" said Eddie. "Not unless you let me play with that dog." He pointed at Jip. "And I want some ice cream, too. I helped make it."

"You can't play with Jip because he belongs to my Aunt Cornelia," Samantha said firmly. "And you can't have any ice cream because it's for my party."

"And *you* are not invited," said Agatha.

"Absolutely not," said Agnes. "This party

is only for girls."

"No boys are allowed," said Agatha. "Isn't that right, girls?"

Everyone chimed in, "Right! No boys are allowed."

"Then I'll keep the bear," said Eddie stubbornly.

"Eddie, you are a nincompoop!" said Agnes.

"Nincompoop!" said all the girls, laughing. It tickled their mouths to say such a funny word. "Eddie is a nincompoop! Eddie is a nincompoop!" they taunted. But before they could say "nincompoop" again, Agatha tackled Eddie around the knees and knocked him to the ground. She ripped the bear out of his hands and ran back through the hedge, with all the girls clapping and cheering behind her in a wild stampede.

The stampede stopped short at the circle of chairs. There stood Grandmary, waiting. "My heavens!" said Grandmary. "Whatever has happened?"

"Oh, Grandmary," panted Samantha. "Jip ran off with the teddy bear and we had to chase him." She didn't mention the part about tackling Eddie, since she *knew* that was breaking Grandmary's rule about fighting.

"I see," said Grandmary. "Well, I hope you weren't making a spectacle of yourselves." She looked around at the out-of-breath girls. Agnes's sash was untied. Agatha had grass stains on her stockings. Samantha's circlet of roses was tilted over one ear, like a halo gone wrong. Ida Dean had lost her hairbow entirely. Grandmary looked almost as if she might smile, but she didn't. Instead, she said, "You ladies seem to be a bit warm from your exercise. Perhaps this is the perfect time to have a cooling drink of lemonade."

Grandmary led the girls up the stairs of the porch to the birthday table. It was set with a beautiful lace cloth, Grandmary's best gold spoons, and a big crystal pitcher of pink lemonade. There was a little nosegay of pink roses at each place. After they sat down, Samantha gave each girl a favor—a lovely lace fan.

The girls tried to act like young ladies again, opening and closing their fans and fluttering them elegantly in front of their faces. They nibbled on thin tea sandwiches and sipped daintily from their goblets of lemonade. When Mrs. Hawkins carried out the tray of ten tiny cakes all glowing with candles, the girls gasped with delight. Everyone sang "Happy Birthday to You" and clapped politely when Samantha blew out all the candles in one whoosh.

"This is such an elegant party," said Agnes as Mrs. Hawkins put one of the petit fours on her plate.

"Would you care for some ice cream?" Samantha asked in her most grown-up voice as Hawkins began serving.

"Oh! Molded ice cream!" chirped Ruth. "Just like in a fancy ice cream parlor!"

"And wait 'til you taste it!" exclaimed Agnes.

All the girls put rather large, unladylike spoonfuls in their mouths. Their faces turned as pink as the ice cream.

"Ugh!"

"Eew!"

"Ick!"

"Awful!"

The girls coughed and choked. They spat the ice cream out into their napkins. They slurped down gulps of lemonade. They clutched their

throats and stuck out their tongues. They sputtered
and gasped and gagged.

"SALT!" said Samantha. "This ice cream is full
of salt!"

Hawkins looked puzzled. "But just a few
minutes ago young Master Eddie tasted it, and he
didn't complain."

"Was Eddie alone with the ice cream?" asked
Samantha.

"Why, yes, I suppose he was," answered
Hawkins. "Just before I put it into the molds."

"That rotten Eddie!" exclaimed Agnes. "He put

salt in the ice cream and ruined it for all of us!"

"Where is he? I'll fix him," threatened Agatha, frowning fiercely. She jumped up and ran smack into Cornelia.

"Whoa!" said Cornelia. "What's the matter, Agatha?" She looked around at the girls. "Why do you all look so sour?"

"Not sour," explained Samantha. "Salty. Eddie Ryland put salt in the ice cream and it's *ruined*."

Aunt Cornelia tasted the ice cream. "My stars!" she said. "You're right!" She looked at the disappointed girls. "Well," she said briskly, "you certainly can't eat *that!* But you still have lovely petit fours and delicious lemonade. Just ignore the ice cream."

All the girls carefully pushed the bowls of salty ice cream toward the center of the table. They ate their petit fours in silence. Samantha could hardly swallow, she felt so angry and sad. Her beautiful, elegant birthday party had been spoiled. But Agnes and Agatha finished eating quickly and hurried away from the table. They whispered with Cornelia for a few moments, then bounded back over to Samantha.

"We have the most wonderful idea!" crowed Agnes. "You're going to come to New York!"

"Ooooh!" sighed all the girls. "New York!"

"Cornelia says if it's all right with Grandmary, you can come to New York and stay at her new house," said Agatha.

"You can come next week," said Agnes. "We'll be there, too, and we can all go to Tyson's Ice Cream Parlor for the best ice cream in New York."

"With no Eddie Ryland to spoil it," said Agatha, the fierce gleam back in her eyes.

"I'd love that," said Samantha. The twins' latest idea made the disappointment of salty ice cream melt away. "May I go?" she asked Grandmary.

"Of course you may," said Grandmary. "And I shall go with you. I've been looking forward to peppermint ice cream myself!"

NEW YORK CITY

New York City! Just the name was
magic! Samantha leaned forward to
peek out of the horse-drawn cab. She
and Grandmary were riding along the busy city
streets from the train station to Gard and Cornelia's
new house. Samantha held on to her hat and
twisted her head around, trying to see to the tops
of the buildings. Everything in New York was so
big! There were so many people hurrying along the
sidewalks. In New York it always seemed as if
something exciting was about to happen.

"I can't wait to see Agnes and Agatha,"
Samantha said to Grandmary.

"You do have a good time with them, don't

you, dear?" said Grandmary.

"They're always so much fun," said Samantha.

"They are happy, lively girls," agreed Grandmary. "Though they do get a bit carried away with their ideas sometimes."

Samantha understood what Grandmary meant about Agnes and Agatha. Sometimes their ideas were as tangled as their bouncy red curls. "They're always thinking up new ways to do things," Samantha went on.

"Yes," said Grandmary. "But I'm afraid they don't always think very carefully. Besides, they don't realize that many times the old ways are still the best ways."

Suddenly, the cab jerked to a stop. Grandmary and Samantha leaned forward to look out. They were stopped at the edge of a big park. The sidewalk was so crowded, people spilled out into the street. Samantha saw some women hanging large banners across the entrance to the park. One banner said "WOMEN, FIGHT FOR YOUR RIGHT TO VOTE." Another banner said "NOW IS THE TIME FOR CHANGE."

"We'll have to go another way, ma'am," the

cab driver called down to Grandmary. "These ladies seem to be blocking traffic all around Madison Square Park."

"Very well, do what you think is best," Grandmary answered. She sat back. She didn't seem to want to look at what was going on.

But Samantha was fascinated. "What's happening here?" she asked Grandmary.

"Well, it appears that a group of women is having a meeting in that park," Grandmary replied.

"Who are they?" Samantha asked.

"They're suffragists," Grandmary answered. "They think women should be able to vote, so they get together and make a ruckus about changing the laws." She sat up very straight. "It's all just new-fangled notions."

The cab turned down a quieter street and Samantha sat back. She was still very curious about the meeting in the park, but she could tell by the look on Grandmary's face that she should not ask any more questions about it.

They rode in silence until the cab stopped in front of Gard and Cornelia's tall, narrow brownstone house. Samantha

208

had just hopped out onto the sidewalk when she heard voices shouting, "Samantha! Samantha!" She looked up. Agnes and Agatha were leaning out of a window high above her, waving wildly. Agnes held up Jip and waved his paw. Jip barked and wriggled with joy.

"Hello!" Samantha called. She skipped and waved, already swept away by the twins' high spirits.

"We'll be right down!" Agatha yelled. Then she and Agnes and Jip disappeared from the window.

Cornelia smiled as she came down the front steps to Samantha and Grandmary. "Welcome!" she said. Just then the twins and Jip came flying out the door and down the steps. "Hurray! You're here!" they said as they hugged Samantha. Aunt Cornelia laughed. "Come in, come in," she said. "As you can see, we're all very glad you're here."

The twins led Samantha into the dark, cool house. Uncle Gard was waiting just inside the doorway. He blinked at Samantha and said, "There you are, Sam! I've been looking for you all week long. I can't seem to find anything in this new house."

"Do you think you could help us find some lunch?" asked Aunt Cornelia.

"Certainly, certainly," said Uncle Gard, kissing the tip of her nose. "When it comes to finding food, I never have any trouble."

"Come on, Samantha!" said Agnes and Agatha. They pulled her into the dining room and made her sit between them. Then, both at once, they began showering her with questions. "Have you seen that terrible Eddie? How was your train ride? Do you want to go to the park after lunch? Do you want—"

"Girls!" Aunt Cornelia scolded gently as the maid began to pass the food. "You'll put Samantha in a spin with all your questions! There will be plenty of time for chatter later. I haven't even had a chance to ask Grandmary where she plans to shop today."

"I'll shop at O'Neill's, of course," replied Grandmary. "I never go any farther."

"There's a fine new shop on Fifth Avenue that's closer than O'Neill's," said Uncle Gard. "What was the name of that store, Cornelia?"

Grandmary patted his arm and smiled. "Don't trouble yourself to remember, Gardner," she said.

"I shall go to O'Neill's. I've shopped there for more than thirty years. I'm too old to change my ways now."

"O'Neill's is near Madison Square Park," said Aunt Cornelia slowly. "That area may be quite crowded today. There's a meeting in the park."

"I know," said Grandmary. "We passed it on our way from the station. Those suffragists were already blocking traffic." She shook her head. "In my opinion, ladies should not gather in public places. *Especially* not to carry on about this voting nonsense."

"Nonsense?" Aunt Cornelia asked. Her voice rose ever so slightly.

"Of course," said Grandmary. "Voting is not a lady's concern. It never has been. I see no reason to change things now. Those suffragists are making spectacles of themselves. They should stay at home where ladies belong."

Samantha saw Agnes and Agatha look at each other with raised eyebrows, then quickly look down into their soup bowls.

Aunt Cornelia opened her mouth to say

211

something, then shut it again.

Samantha was bursting with curiosity. "But why—?" she began to ask.

"Well, well, well," interrupted Uncle Gard. "Well, well. The strangest thing happened to me as I was walking home from work the other day. A man came up to me and said, 'Do you know any girls who just turned ten years old?' And I said, 'Why, yes, in fact I do know one.' And he said, 'Would you give her this large box? There's something inside she might like.' So I brought the box home. It's out in the hall. Perhaps you'll open it, Sam, and show us what's inside."

Samantha forgot all about her questions. She and the twins ran from the table and opened the door. Jip was waiting right outside. He barked and jumped as the twins helped Samantha tear off the wrapping paper and open the box. Inside was a pram—the prettiest doll carriage Samantha had ever seen. It was deep red with shiny brass wheels. "Jiminy!" Samantha whispered. "It's beautiful!" She ran to give Uncle Gard a big hug. "Thank you, Uncle Gard! Thank you very much!" She knew perfectly well the doll carriage was from Uncle Gard and no one else.

"Let's take it to Gramercy Park right now!" suggested Agnes.

"That *would* be fun!" Samantha said eagerly. "May we go?"

"Certainly!" said Uncle Gard.

"Can Jip come, too?" asked Agatha. "You know how he loves the park."

"No, I don't think that is a good idea," said Aunt Cornelia. "Remember what happened at Samantha's party when he ran away from you?"

"Oh, but nothing like that will happen *here*," said Agatha quickly. "The park has a fence all around it."

"Please, please, please?" begged Agnes.

Aunt Cornelia thought for a moment.

"We'll only be across the street in the park," wheedled Agatha.

"And you won't go any farther than that?" asked Aunt Cornelia.

"No!" the twins promised together.

"Will you keep Jip on his leash?"

"Yes!" shouted the girls.

"Promise?"

"Absolutely!" they cried.

"Well, all right," Cornelia finally agreed. "But—"

"Hurray!" the twins interrupted. Jip began yipping in excitement.

"Please be calm for just a minute," Aunt Cornelia said seriously. "I'm going to a meeting, but I'll be back at three-thirty. When I get back, we'll walk to the ice cream parlor to meet Grandmary. Don't forget."

"And don't forget to behave like young ladies," added Grandmary.

"And don't forget the rule about keeping Jip on the leash," repeated Aunt Cornelia.

"And don't forget to have a good time," said Uncle Gard, shaking his finger at them.

"We won't!" said the girls. And Jip barked to show that he agreed.

C H A P T E R
F O U R
—

FOLLOW THAT DOG!

 Jip led a very cheerful parade to
Gramercy Park. He pranced along
the sidewalk, pulling at his leash.
Agnes and Agatha skipped to keep up with him.
Samantha followed behind, proudly pushing her
new doll carriage. Even the doll Agnes had loaned
her, which was rather tired-looking, seemed to perk
up as she rode in the fine red pram out in the
midday sunshine.

Gramercy Park was a pretty rectangular green
across the street from Gard and Cornelia's house.
It was fenced on all four sides by tall black iron
railings with two locked gates. The buildings that
surrounded it seemed to look down on the quiet

little park fondly, as if they wanted to protect it from the hubbub of the city.

Agnes unlocked one gate, and the girls followed Jip into the park. He zigzagged from one side of the path to the other, sniffing out interesting scents as he led the girls to a large fountain in the center of the park. Around the bottom of the fountain there was a pool where tin swans swam. "How pretty," said Samantha. "The swans look almost real."

Jip seemed to agree with Samantha. He growled at the swans and dragged on his leash, trying to get at them.

"Stop it, Jip," scolded Agatha, jerking him back. She tried to pull Jip away, but he lunged and leaped, barking wildly all the while. "Jip's pulling my arm out," complained Agatha.

"You'd better carry him," suggested Samantha.

So Agatha picked Jip up, but he kept barking even when they walked away from the fountain. When Agatha put him down, Jip tried to run back to the swans, so she had to pick him up again. He squirmed in her arms. "I'm tired of carrying Jip," Agatha whined. "You take him, Agnes."

"Absolutely not," said Agnes. "He'll get paw prints all over my dress. I don't want to be a mess like you are. After all," she said in a hoity-toity voice, "ladies do not make spectacles of themselves."

Samantha had to laugh. Agnes sounded just like Grandmary.

"Well, it's not fair," grumbled Agatha. "I've carried Jip enough. It was your dumb idea to bring him."

"It was not," said Agnes.

"It was too," said Agatha.

"It was not."

"It was too."

"Oh, *I'll* carry him," Samantha said firmly. "You push the pram, Agatha."

Agatha eyed the doll carriage. "No," she said. "I have a better idea."

"What now?" asked Agnes.

"Let's put Jip in the pram. That way none of us will have to carry him," said Agatha.

Agnes was instantly enthusiastic. "Oh, that *is* a good idea!" she said. "He can sit right next to the doll."

But Samantha didn't think it sounded like such a good idea. "We promised Cornelia we wouldn't let Jip off the leash," she reminded the twins.

"We're not going to let *Jip* off the leash," said Agatha. "We're going to let *me* off the leash. Just watch." Agatha slipped the leash off her wrist and put Jip in the pram. She looped the leash over the handle of the pram. "There! You see?" she said. "He's perfectly safe."

Samantha shook her head. "I don't think—"

Agnes interrupted, "Oh, don't be such a worrywart, Samantha. This is a brand-new way to walk a dog. It's a great idea. Doesn't Jip look cute?"

And Jip did look cute, but only for one second. He yanked the leash with his mouth and pulled it off the handle. Then, before the girls could grab him, he leaped out of the carriage and took off like a streak.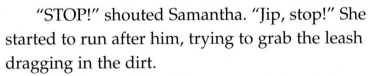

"STOP!" shouted Samantha. "Jip, stop!" She started to run after him, trying to grab the leash dragging in the dirt.

"Jip! Jip! Jip! Jip! Jip!" Agatha yelped. She hopped up and down, waving her arms.

"Oh, no!" wailed all three girls when they saw Jip wiggle between the iron bars of the fence and slip out of the park. Just for a second, he turned to look at them.

"What'll we do now?" groaned Agnes. "Cornelia will be furious!"

"Quick! Climb over the fence!" yelled Agatha wildly. She ran to the fence and started to shinny up the iron bars. "Split up! Get the firemen! Call the police!"

Agnes just stood still, holding her face in her hands, moaning.

Samantha saw that she was going to have to take charge. "Don't just stand there!" she ordered. "We've got to catch him! Come on!" She led the twins to the gate and pushed it open. They could see Jip halfway down the block, his white tail waving like a feather as he trotted along. The gate swung shut behind them.

"Your doll carriage!" cried Agnes.

"Leave it," Samantha said as she ran. "We've *got* to get Jip!"

The three girls took off after Jip. He was running toward a big hotel on the corner. Samantha

As the girls dashed after Jip,
Samantha heard a frightening rumble overhead.

saw a group of people waiting in front with piles
of luggage around them. "Stop that dog!" she called.
But Jip was too fast. He bounded through the
crowd, jumped over a trunk, and slipped around
the corner.

As the girls dashed after him, Samantha heard
a frightening rumble. A shower of soot fell like
black snow. She looked up for one second to see a
train running along a track built up over the street.
When she looked down again, Jip had disappeared.

"Where'd he go?" she gasped to Agnes.

"I don't know," Agnes wailed. "We've lost him.
Forever and ever!"

"Not if I can help it!" said Samantha. She ran
up to a man pushing a cart full of strawberries.
"Have you seen our dog?" she asked urgently.

"Yes, yes!" said the man. "He went that way."
He pointed farther up the street.

"Thanks!" yelled Samantha.

"There he is!" shouted Agatha. They saw
Jip's tail bouncing along ahead of a wagon over-
flowing with flowers. The wagon looked just
like Grandmary's garden in Mount Bedford. But
chasing Jip in New York City was a lot different

from chasing him in Mount Bedford. The city was so big, and Jip was so little. What if they lost him? What if—

Clang! Clang! Clang!

Samantha practically jumped out of her skin as a big streetcar rumbled up to the curb in front of her. The huge, sweaty horses that pulled it shook their harnesses, snorting as they waited for people to get off. Samantha looked at the heavy hooves and thought how easily Jip could be crushed by them.

"Now where is he?" cried Agnes.

"I see him," said Agatha. "On the other side of the street."

The girls dashed across the street, weaving between a wagon full of rattling milk cans and an automobile whose horn blared at them. Jip was far ahead of them now, slithering like a snake through the crowd. It was hard for the girls to move very fast because the sidewalk was so full of people. The girls had to wiggle their way between fashionable ladies, gentlemen in straw hats, boys selling newspapers, and workmen carrying heavy loads. "'Scuse me, 'scuse me," said Samantha as she and the twins jostled past the people.

Agatha tripped over a loose brick in the sidewalk and fell to her knees. "Ow!" she wailed, almost in tears. She knelt on the sidewalk. "Go ahead, leave me behind."

"No," said Samantha. She helped Agatha get up and dusted her off. "You're fine. Come on," she said. "You can't stop now. We need you. You're the best one at spotting Jip."

None of them saw Jip again until they got to the corner of Fifth Avenue, the widest and busiest street in New York. "Look!" called Agatha, pointing with both hands. "There's Jip! In the street!"

Samantha leaped off the curb to get him when suddenly the pavement shook beneath her feet. Someone yanked her back up onto the sidewalk. She was almost crushed in the tumble of people who scrambled to get back on the curb. "Watch out!" a voice shouted. "Fire engine! Out of the way!"

"JIP!" yelled Samantha. She caught a glimpse of Jip, but then two huge horses galloped in front of her, pulling a fire engine. Its deafening bell rang out over the shouts and screams from the crowd. The firemen clung to the shiny pump in the middle of the wagon as it stormed past in a blur of red and silver, stirring up a cloud of dust in the street, racing like the wind.

"Jip," Samantha whispered. Was Jip somewhere in that cloud of dust? Nothing moved in the street. "Oh, Jip, we never should have let you go."

CHANGES

The fire engine roared off around the corner. The dust settled. Samantha stood on the curb, gathering her courage to go out into the street and look for Jip.

Agnes and Agatha ran up to her. "Where is he?" Agnes asked breathlessly. "Where's Jip? Do you see him?"

Samantha shook her head no. "I think he might . . . he might be . . ."

"There he is!" shouted Agatha, hopping up and down. "Look! He's going into that park across the street."

"I see him!" shouted Samantha. She was so relieved. "Come on! Now we've *got* to catch him."

The girls dashed across the street into the park. Jip trip-trotted ahead of them as if he knew exactly where he was going and nothing would stop him. He darted through a crowd of women who were all headed toward a platform draped with signs and flags.

"Oh, no!" Agnes gulped. "This is Madison Square Park, where the suffragists' meeting is!"

"Quick! Let's get out of here!" said Agatha in a panic.

"No," said Samantha. "We've got to get Jip. Grandmary won't mind if we're in the park for just a minute to get the dog."

"It's not Grandmary we're worried about," interrupted Agnes. "It's Cornelia. She's here. And if she sees us, she'll be furious. She thinks we're back in Gramercy Park."

"Cornelia?" Samantha gasped. "What's *she* doing here?"

"She's at the meeting about women voting," Agatha said quickly. "We heard her tell Gard she was coming. He said Grandmary wouldn't like it. But Cornelia said she could think for herself and she was coming anyway."

Samantha was very confused. What was
Cornelia doing with the suffragists? Grandmary
said these women were making spectacles of
themselves. Was Cornelia doing something wrong?
But Samantha didn't have time to think. Agnes
grabbed her arm. "Come on!" she ordered. "Let's
get Jip and *go*."

The girls chased Jip to a small pool with a
fountain in the middle. He eyed the girls. As they
came closer, he edged away. "Give him some room,"
said Samantha. "We don't want him to—"

Splash! Jip jumped into the pool!

"I'll dive in and get him!" Agatha cried. She
pulled off her shoe.

"WAIT!" said Samantha quickly. She grabbed
Agatha's shoe and waved it in front of Jip, just as
she had in Mount Bedford. "Look, Jip," she said in
a friendly voice. "A shoe. Come and get it."

Jip looked at the shoe. He began to paddle
across the pool toward Samantha. Just then, the
crowd got very quiet. "Ladies and gentlemen," a
woman's voice began.

Jip stopped. He tilted his head and perked up
his ears. When the speaker said "Welcome," Jip

yelped with joy. He sprang out of the pool, splattering water all over the girls. Before they could grab him, he scampered up the steps of the speakers' platform, yipping and yapping wildly. He ran right up to the woman who was standing in front of everyone.

"CORNELIA!" gasped all three girls. The speaker was Cornelia! Jip wiggled from head to tail, sending a spray of water all over her.

"Jip? What are you doing here?" Cornelia asked. Jip barked excitedly, and she scooped him up in her arms. "Well," she said, turning to the crowd, "this eager fellow wants to speak, too!"

The crowd clapped and laughed.

Cornelia's voice was strong and firm as she went on. "The time has come for all of us to speak out. We must stand up for what we believe is right!" she said. "We must make up our own minds. The time has come to change the old ways. Women *must* vote!"

The crowd clapped louder than ever. Some women waved banners and cheered. Cornelia carried Jip back to her seat, and another woman rose

"CORNELIA!" gasped all three girls.
The speaker was Cornelia!

230

to speak. As Cornelia sat down, she looked all around, searching for faces in the crowd.

"Jeepers! She's looking for us!" whispered Agnes.

"Well, she's got Jip, so let's get out of here!" said Agatha.

"No," said Samantha. "We can't do that. We have to face her and admit what we did."

The twins looked at each other uncomfortably.

"Maybe you're right," sighed Agatha.

The girls waited nervously while other suffragists spoke. When all the speeches were over and the crowd had begun to wander away, Cornelia came down from the platform. She walked toward the girls. "Well," she said without a trace of her usual smile. "What are *you*—and Jip—doing here?"

The girls looked down at their shoes. "We did a very stupid thing," Samantha began.

"It was really a terrible idea," admitted Agnes.

"We put Jip in the pram," said Samantha. "And we didn't hold on to the leash, so he ran away."

Agatha burst out, "But we didn't think that he'd—"

"You certainly *didn't* think," Cornelia cut in. "You just went right ahead with your own ideas and didn't pay any attention to what I said about keeping Jip on the leash. That was an important rule and one we all agreed on. When will you girls learn that you can't just change things when you feel like it?"

"But aren't you trying to change things?" asked Agatha. "Aren't you trying to get women to vote?"

"That's very different, Agatha," answered Cornelia. "All the women here today have thought long and hard about changing the laws so that women can vote. When you want to change something, you'd better be sure it's a wise change, a change for the better."

The girls were silent. Finally Samantha said, "We're very sorry, Aunt Cornelia. We really are."

Cornelia shook her head. "I believe you are sorry," she said. "You certainly look sorry. In fact, you look like a sorry mess." Her voice had a little laugh in it. She looked at her watch. "Oh, my gracious! It's nearly three-thirty. We'll be late meeting Grandmary if we don't leave right now. There's no time to go home and change. We'll have to go to Tyson's as untidy as we are."

The girls were rumpled and wrinkled, and Cornelia's dress was covered with muddy paw prints, so it was a very bedraggled parade that Jip led to the ice cream parlor. When they got to Tyson's, Samantha saw Grandmary sitting at a corner table near the gleaming soda fountain. Her face was rather red, and Samantha was afraid she might be angry.

Samantha rushed ahead of Cornelia and the twins. "Grandmary," she blurted out, "we're sorry to be so late and sorry that we look so messy, but we've had the most awful time. Agnes and Agatha and I nearly lost Jip. We chased him every-where, and finally he ran into Madison Square Park. Remember, the place where the cab stopped this morning? Jip jumped into a fountain there, and just when we almost caught him, he got away again. But it was all right because he ran onto the speakers' platform and right up to—" Samantha stopped. "Oh, no," she said. She didn't want to tell Grandmary about Cornelia.

But Cornelia finished for Samantha. "Jip ran

*"Grandmary," Samantha blurted out, "we're sorry to be so late
and sorry that we look so messy, but we've had the most awful time."*

right up to *me*," she said, looking Grandmary straight in the eye. "*I* was on the speakers' platform."

"I know you were on the platform," said Grandmary. "I saw you. I was at the meeting myself."

"You were?" everyone gasped.

"Yes," said Grandmary firmly. "I was on my way here to Tyson's. But there were so many people around the park that I couldn't get by. When I saw *you* up on the platform, Cornelia, I thought perhaps I ought to stay and listen." Grandmary took Cornelia's hand. "My dear," she said, "I must admit that what I saw and what I heard gave me a bit of a surprise. I've always said that I'm too old to change my ways, but I've changed my mind today."

Grandmary touched her forehead with her handkerchief. Samantha saw that her hat was tipped back a little, as if she'd turned around very suddenly. "You and the other ladies who spoke today were simply saying that women should stand up for what they think is right. That's exactly what I believe, too. And if that's what voting will give us a chance to do, then I think women *should* vote. The time for change *has* come."

Cornelia smiled at Grandmary. "Yes, it is time to change the old rules," she said. "And that's what makes this a wonderful time for these young ladies to be growing up."

"Well, growing up is what we've come to celebrate, isn't it?" asked Grandmary. "Shall we have our ice cream?"

She turned to Samantha. "Peppermint for you, my dear? Or would you like to try something new today?"

"No, thank you," smiled Samantha. "Peppermint is my old favorite. There are some things that are just too good to change."

TO
CHARLOTTE KATHLEEN CAMPBELL
AND
PATRICK GRANGER CAMPBELL

Samantha

SAVES THE DAY

By VALERIE TRIPP

PINEY POINT

Too-oot! With a cheerful blast of its
whistle, the little steamboat chugged
across Goose Lake toward Samantha.
Its snappy red and white awning flapped in the
breeze. Samantha skipped on her tiptoes at the end
of the dock, waving both arms wildly to welcome
the boat and its passengers.

"Yoo-hoo! Hello!" she called. "Agnes! Agatha!
Hello!" As the boat came closer, Samantha could
see Agnes and Agatha standing on the deck,
waving hello to her. Their red curls were as bright
as poppies in the sunshine. The twins were coming
to stay at Piney Point, Grandmary's summer home
in the mountains. Uncle Gard and Aunt Cornelia

were with them. And so was Admiral Archibald Beemis. He came all the way from England every summer to visit Grandmary. Samantha danced with excitement. It was wonderful to have all of her favorite people together at her favorite place in the world. They would be just like a big happy family!

The boat pulled up to the dock, and Agnes and Agatha jumped ashore.

"Samantha!" they cried together. "Hello!" They swooped up to hug her. "We're finally here!"

"Agatha was seasick," announced Agnes.

"I was *not*," protested Agatha.

"She was too," Agnes went on. "And we weren't even on the boat yet. We were on the sleeper train from Albany and . . ."

"Girls!" laughed Aunt Cornelia as she kissed Samantha hello. "Tell Samantha later. Right now you'd better scoot out of the way of the luggage."

The girls stepped back as the boatmen unloaded satchels and trunks, wicker baskets, and suitcases onto the dock. Uncle Gard and Admiral Beemis appeared behind the enormous pile of luggage. Uncle Gard was trying to carry two hatboxes, a parasol, and a picnic hamper. "Pardon

"Samantha!" Agnes and Agatha cried together. "We're finally here!"

me, miss," he said to Samantha. "Did I get off at
the wrong stop? Is this Grand Central Station,
New York?"

"No!" giggled Samantha. "It's Piney Point,
Uncle Gard. Finally, finally everyone's here at
Piney Point."

"Right-oh!" boomed the Admiral. He beamed
with delight and saluted Samantha. His twinkly
eyes were as blue as the lake.

Samantha saluted back with a grin. "Welcome
ashore, Admiral," she said. "Grandmary will be so
happy to see you. We've both been waiting all
morning. Let's go up to the house."

Samantha led everyone up the steep hillside
to the house. The twins exclaimed happily each
step of the way.

"It's so cool here!"

"It smells like Christmas trees!"

"Oooh! Look! A log cabin! It's huge!"

Grandmary was standing
on the shady porch of the
big log house. She looked as
cool and serene as a cloud
in her white summer dress.

"Welcome to Piney Point, my dears," she said
to the twins. "Gardner, Cornelia, hello!" She smiled
as she held out her hand to the Admiral. "Archie!
How lovely to see you!"

"Lovely indeed!" repeated the Admiral. "Mary,
you look as lovely as the day I met you, more than
thirty years ago." He bowed over her hand and
kissed it.

Grandmary laughed, a little pink in the cheeks.
"Oh, Archie, I am glad you're here. It doesn't seem
like summer until you arrive."

"Summer it is," said Uncle Gard. "And I feel as
boiled as a summer squash after that trip. Who's for
a swim?"

"Me!" cried all the girls together.

"All right," said Uncle Gard. He was already
loosening his tie. "I'll meet you at the lake in five
minutes. Last one in is a rotten egg."

"Come on," Samantha said to the twins. "Let's
go and change."

"Wait," said Agnes as she followed Samantha
down the porch steps. "Where are we going? We
don't have to live out in the woods, do we?"

Samantha grinned. "No. One of the best things

about Piney Point is that we all have our own little houses. The Admiral stays over the boathouse. Uncle Gard and Aunt Cornelia are in the Rose Cottage. And *this* is ours." She flung open the door to a one-room cottage. It had three tall windows facing the lake. Samantha had filled big baskets with goldenrod and black-eyed Susans. Their fresh, woodsy scent filled the little house.

"Is this house for the three of us?" asked Agatha. "Just us and no grownups?"

"That's right," said Samantha. "Just us."

"I absolutely love it!" sighed Agnes. She flopped onto one of the three beds and looked around. "Look at that chair made out of tree branches. The branches are so shiny and twisted together, the chair looks like it's made out of pretzels."

"Our little house is like a treehouse," said Agatha as she leaned out a window into the waving branches of a pine tree. "Does it have a name, too?"

"Mmm hmm," answered Samantha. She was pulling her bathing suit over her head. "It's called

Wood Tick Inn."

"Wood *Tick?*" asked Agnes uncertainly. She sat up suddenly and looked into the corners of the room. "Ticks are bugs, aren't they? Is it called Wood Tick Inn because it's full of horrible bugs?"

"No!" laughed Samantha. "Not horrible bugs. But you *might* see a few ladybugs or spiders—"

"Spiders?" Agnes clutched her bathing suit to her chest.

"Oh, honestly, Agnes," said Agatha as she pulled off her long stockings. "You're not in the city now. This is the wilderness. There's *supposed* to be wildlife here. We'll probably see lots of bears and wolves and hear coyotes howling in the night. Isn't that right, Samantha?"

"Well, I've never seen any bears or wolves," said Samantha. "But there are lots of other animals to see, like deer and moose and rabbits. And the lake is full of fish."

"Do the fish bite?" asked Agnes.

"Of course not!" said Samantha. "Unless your toes look like worms! Come on! Let's go swimming!" She led the twins down a path covered with pine needles to the edge of the water.

"Look!" said Agatha. "Gard and the Admiral are out on that big rock in the lake. Let's swim to them."

"All right!" agreed Samantha.

"I think I'll just wade," said Agnes. She timidly put one toe in the water.

"I don't know what's the matter with her," said Agatha as she and Samantha splashed into the lake. "She's brave enough in the city, but here she acts like a scaredy-cat about little things like bugs and fish. Really!"

"Don't worry," said Samantha. "She'll get over it. Nobody stays fussy or scared at Piney Point. Come on! I'll race you to the rock."

And Samantha was absolutely right. Piney Point quickly worked its magic on Agnes. In just a few days, she was splashing straight into the lake, right along with the other girls. When the Admiral took them trout fishing, Agnes even put the worms on the hook with her own fingers.

Every day at Piney Point was filled with wonderful things to discover. In the morning

Mrs. Hawkins gave the girls sandwiches to put in their pack baskets, and off they went exploring. Samantha showed Agnes and Agatha where sweet red raspberries grew on the hillside. She led them to a sunny meadow where they caught butterflies with their long-handled nets. The three girls canoed to the marsh. There turtles sunned themselves on the rocks, noisy birds nested in the cattails, and frogs poked just their eyes out of the water. One day they saw a mother deer and her fawn very near their house, and once they watched a big elk drinking out of the lake.

From early morning, when the gauzy mist rose off the lake, until late at night when lightning bugs twinkled all around them like falling stars, the girls were so happy and busy that the long summer days just flew past. After two weeks at Piney Point, the twins' noses were sprinkled with freckles and their hair was golden orange. So the Admiral called them "the Tiger Lilies."

The Admiral was one of the best parts of Piney Point. Each afternoon he joined Samantha, Agnes, and Agatha for a swim. He paddled along with his

head raised out of the water, like a duck.
Sometimes he invited the girls along when he took
Grandmary out rowing in the moonlight. He gave
Samantha a genuine bo's'n's whistle
made of shiny brass and taught her
how to blow signals like the sailors
did. And he gave all three girls
sailor hats, which they proudly
wore whenever they went boating on the lake.

One hot, still day, the girls were picking
wildflowers on the rocky hill behind the main
house. Samantha raced ahead of the twins and
scrambled up to the top of a big boulder. She held
an imaginary spyglass up to one eye and looked all
around her. "Who am I?" she asked Agatha.

"You're Admiral Archibald Beemis!" Agatha
cried. She climbed up on the boulder next to
Samantha.

"Right-oh!" Samantha replied with a salute.

"Gosh," panted Agnes as she climbed up on
the rock, too. "You can see all over from up here.
You can really see why they call it Goose Lake.
Over there is the goose's thin neck, and there's its
head. That big island is its eye."

"Look at that pretty little
island just below the goose's eye," said
Agatha. "What's that called, Samantha?"

"That's Teardrop Island," Samantha
answered. She climbed down from the boulder.

"Oh, because it's shaped like a teardrop,"
Agnes said.

"Do you see that rocky cliff?" asked Agatha.
She pointed to a cliff at the end of Teardrop Island.
"I'd love to climb that. I bet you can see all the
way to New York from there."

"I have a great idea!" exclaimed Agnes. "Let's
go to Teardrop Island tomorrow. We can go in the
canoe and take a picnic and stay all day!"

"That would be fun," agreed Agatha. "We
could bring our paints, too."

"No," said Samantha.

But the twins didn't hear her. "We can be real
explorers," Agatha went on. "We can hike from one
end of the island to the other."

"No," Samantha said again, louder. "I don't
want to go there."

The twins were surprised. "Why not?"

"Because it's . . . it's not a good place," said

Samantha. She pushed her sweaty bangs off her forehead.

"But it looks so pretty," said Agatha. "What's the matter with it?"

"Are there bears and wolves on the island?" asked Agnes. "Is it dangerous?"

"The island isn't dangerous, but you have to go through that narrow part of the lake to get there," said Samantha. "It's filled with big sharp rocks."

"We can steer around those rocks," said Agatha. "That's easy!"

"The dangerous rocks are hidden underwater. You can't see them, but they can still rip out the bottom of your boat," said Samantha. She was quiet for a moment. Then she said softly, "That's where my mother and father drowned. There was a storm, and their boat was wrecked on the rocks. They were on their way back from Teardrop Island."

"Oh!" said both twins. They looked very sad.

"That's terrible, Samantha," said Agatha quietly. "That's just terrible."

"We're sorry," said Agnes. "We didn't know about . . . about what happened there. We didn't mean to make you feel bad, Samantha, really we didn't."

"I know," said Samantha. She bent down to pick some wildflowers growing near the boulder. "It's just that I hate to even think about Teardrop Island. It makes me sad, and scared, too. I never want to go there. Not *ever*."

"I don't want to go there either," said Agatha.

"Me either," said Agnes. "Besides, there are plenty of other places we can go and things we can do."

"That's right!" agreed Agatha. "There are millions of things to do at Piney Point. Come on! Let's go swimming. It's too hot to pick any more flowers."

"We'll race you," said Agnes. She grabbed Samantha's hand. "Come on, Samantha!"

The three girls ran very fast down the hill toward the shining blue lake.

That night it was still very hot. The Admiral helped the girls drag their mattresses out to the little porch on Wood Tick Inn so they could sleep out in the soft, warm breeze from the lake. There was a patch of velvety black sky above them, framed by the tops of pine trees. Hundreds of stars glittered and winked at them.

The girls stretched out on their backs with their heads together. "There are lots more stars here than there are in the city," said Agnes.

"And they're much closer," said Agatha.

"Mmm," agreed Samantha.

The girls could hear waves lapping peacefully against the shore. The murmur of the adults' voices drifted up from the porch of the main house where Grandmary, Uncle Gard, Aunt Cornelia, and the Admiral sat to catch the breeze. Once in a while, the murmur turned into laughter. The girls could hear the Admiral's loud, hearty "Haw! Haw!"

Samantha smiled. "I love the way the Admiral laughs. He sounds like a happy donkey."

"He's the best grownup I've ever met," stated Agnes. "He's not afraid of anything. He's not bossy. And he knows interesting things. He knows more about this place than anyone."

"He's been coming here a long time," said Samantha. "He was my grandfather's best friend.

After Grandpa died, he kept coming anyway, all the way from England, every summer." She rolled over onto her stomach. "Can you keep a secret?" she whispered.

"Yes!" exclaimed the twins. They rolled over onto their stomachs, too, and wiggled up close to Samantha.

"Well," Samantha whispered, "I heard Mrs. Hawkins tell Elsa once that every summer the Admiral asks Grandmary to marry him."

"Gosh," breathed the twins, delighted with the secret.

"I guess Grandmary always says no," sighed Agatha. "I wonder why."

"Doesn't she like him?" asked Agnes.

"I don't know," said Samantha. "I think she likes him a lot."

"Well," said Agnes definitely, "if they ever did get married, you'd have a great grandfather."

"You mean a step-grandfather," corrected Agatha.

"I mean a grandfather who is great," said Agnes. "I think the Admiral would be the best grandfather in the world."

"So do I," said Samantha. She put her cheek down on her hands and closed her eyes. The soft breeze soon sang her to sleep.

CHAPTER
TWO
—

THE SKETCHBOOK

A dreary gray sky hung over the girls the next morning. During breakfast, it started to rain. The rain fell hard and heavy, swooping in sheets across the lake, ribboning down the windowpanes. By midmorning the ground looked like soupy chocolate pudding.

Agnes moaned, "How can it rain so hard? The sky was perfectly clear last night."

"The weather can change very quickly here on these mountain lakes," said the Admiral. "Sunny one minute, rainy the next." He peered out the window. "We're in for it today. This is a real summer storm. Time to batten down the hatches! Foul weather ahead!"

The three girls just looked at him with faces as mopey as the moose over the mantel. "It's only eleven o'clock in the morning and we've already done absolutely everything there is to do," complained Samantha. It was true. They had helped Mrs. Hawkins make bread. They had been shooed out of Wood Tick Inn by a maid who wanted to dust. They had watched the boatman fix the big red canoe in the boathouse. They had pressed every wildflower they'd gathered the day before. Agatha had finished embroidering the tiny pillow she'd stuffed with pine needles from the evergreen trees. Samantha had rearranged all the postcards in her album. Agnes had worked on jigsaw puzzles for hours. The three girls had run out of indoor things to do.

"Well," said the Admiral cheerily, "since we can't go fishing we might as well play Old Maid, eh what?"

And so until lunchtime, the girls and the Admiral played game after game of Old Maid. The Admiral lost every game, mostly because he was so nice. "I say, Samantha," he'd exclaim. "I've just picked up the Old Maid." So everyone always knew when he had it in his hand.

After lunch the grownups all took naps. "How can they be tired when they haven't done anything all day?" Agatha wondered out loud. She plunked herself down on the bearskin rug in front of the fire.

"I'm bored," complained Agnes. "I wish we could go outside."

"I have an idea!" said Samantha. "Let's set up our easels and paint on the porch. That way we can be outdoors and not get wet."

"Good idea!" said Agatha. "I'm going to paint a picture of you, Samantha."

It was a little windy on the porch and rather damp, but it felt good to get out of the house. The three artists got out their wooden boxes filled with tubes of paint and worked happily and quietly for a while.

Then Agatha looked over at Agnes's easel. "Jeepers, Agnes," she said. "That's an awfully big rabbit you're painting."

"It's not a rabbit," said Agnes. "It's a sailboat."

"Oh," said Agatha. "How come it has ears?"

"Those aren't ears," said Agnes crossly. "That's supposed to be a flag." She sighed. "I have a little trouble making the paint go where I want it to go."

"I know what you mean," said Samantha. "This house I'm painting looks as if a giant had stepped on it and squooshed it."

The girls giggled.

"Maybe there's something wrong with these paintbrushes," said Agatha. She looked at the bristles of her brush. "Maybe they're worn out."

"Grandmary told me there are more brushes in the attic," said Samantha. "Let's go look for them."

Samantha led the way up the wide stairs to the second floor. They tiptoed past Grandmary's door so they wouldn't disturb her nap, and climbed up the narrow stairs to the attic.

The attic was long and dark. It smelled of dried flowers and dust.

"It's spooky up here," whispered Agnes. And it was, just a little. In the corners there were old chairs covered with sheets, so they looked like lumpy ghosts. Outside, the wind swished through the treetops. The rain had calmed down to a steady, soaking shower. It sounded unhurried, as if it would stay forever. The light from the windows was so murky, the girls couldn't tell what time of day it was, or even what season.

"Oooh, look!" cried Agatha. "Old hats! Boxes and boxes of them!" The girls threw off the dusty lids and lifted the hats out of tissue paper. The hats were old-fashioned and frilly. They had big floppy brims and wide satin ribbons. Agnes found one with a whole bird on top, and Samantha found one with an enormous pink bow. They put the hats on

and paraded in front of a greenish mirror that sent
back a wavery image.

They found gloves in another box, and beads,
handbags, and shoes. In one box they found a stiff
corset. Beneath a pile of old riding boots, Samantha
found a box of photo albums and scrapbooks. The
leather books were shut fast with brass clasps. Their
gold-edged pages looked as if no one had turned
them in a long, long time.

Samantha sat on the floor and opened one of
the heavy books. The pictures were brown and
yellow and a little faded. Everyone looked very
stiff and solemn.

"What is that?" asked Agatha. She sat down
next to Samantha.

"It's one of Grandmary's old photograph
albums," answered Samantha. "Jiminy! Here's a
picture of Uncle Gard when he was
little. Look at his long curls!"

"He's as roly-poly as a teddy
bear," laughed Agatha.

"There he is with a fish he
caught. That was taken right here,
on the dock at Piney Point," said

Agnes. She was looking over Samantha's shoulder. "The fish is as big as he is!"

The girls fell into fits of giggles and sneezes from the dust.

"Is that you, Samantha?" asked Agnes, pointing to a dark-haired girl in one of the old pictures.

"No," said Samantha. "That must be my mother when she was a girl. See, it's labeled 'Lydia.'" She stared hard at the face that smiled at her from the picture.

"She looks just like you," said Agatha. "Her smile is the same as yours."

"Do you miss her and your father just awfully?" asked Agnes.

"I miss them, but I don't really remember them very much," said Samantha. "They died when I was only five." She sighed. "I wish I *could* remember more about them and the things we did together, but I really can't."

Agatha turned to the last photograph in the book. "Here's your mother again, with Grandmary. And that man must be your grandfather. Look at Uncle Gard, pretending to steer the boat!"

All three girls smiled at silly Uncle Gard.

"These pictures are funny," said Agnes. "I wonder why Grandmary keeps them hidden away up here."

"Maybe they make her sad," said Samantha. "Maybe they make her miss my mother and grandpa too much." She put the big book back in the box and pulled out a smaller maroon one. On the cover, it said "My Sketchbook." Inside, on the first page, someone had written "Happy Memories of Teardrop Island" and, below that, "Sketches and Watercolors by Lydia."

"What's this book?" asked Agatha. Her curls brushed Samantha's cheek as she leaned forward to look.

Samantha turned the pages slowly. "It looks like something my mother made," she said. "It's sketches and watercolors of Teardrop Island."

"She was a really good artist," said Agnes.

The girls were quiet as they looked through the book. There were tiny, perfect drawings of birds and squirrels, trees and butterflies. There were larger watercolor paintings, too. The colors were soft and shimmery, as if they came through the mist of a rainbow.

Near the middle of the book there was a picture that showed a little bare-legged girl standing in a shallow pool of water. She was holding on to a man's hands

Samantha at the waterfall, 1897

and smiling. Behind them was a tangle of wild roses and a beautiful waterfall tumbling down over mossy rocks. The sunlight poured through the trees, and its greenish light made the scene look like a fairyland. At the bottom of the picture it said, "Samantha at the waterfall, 1897."

"Oh, that's you!" breathed Agnes. "With your father!"

"Look at the waterfall," said Agatha. "Was it really that beautiful?"

"I don't know," said Samantha. She shook her head. "I don't remember anything about it. I didn't even know I'd ever been to Teardrop Island."

"But look," said Agnes. "The whole rest of the book is filled with pictures of you and your parents on Teardrop Island. You're having picnics and picking flowers . . ." She flipped through the pages. "It seems like it was your favorite place. It looks like your parents took you there lots of times."

At the bottom of the picture it said,
"Samantha at the waterfall, 1897."

Samantha stared and stared at the drawings. She had always thought Teardrop Island was a dark, sad place. But in her mother's drawings it was lovely and full of light. Teardrop Island didn't look like a place to be afraid of or a place to hate at all. Samantha turned back to the painting of the waterfall. She could almost smell the roses and feel the slippery, mossy stones under her feet. *My parents and I were together there,* she thought. *And we looked so happy!*

Suddenly she said, "Let's go there. Let's go to Teardrop Island."

Agnes and Agatha looked up at her. "But I thought you didn't want to go there, *ever*," said Agatha.

"Well, I didn't know it was so beautiful," said Samantha. "And I didn't know I used to go there with my mother and father. I forgot. Maybe if I go back, I'll remember. I'll remember what it was like . . . and what my parents were like . . . and being together . . ." She smoothed the page under her hand. "I just have to go there. Do you want to come with me?"

"Of course!" said both twins.

"We'll go tomorrow," said Samantha. "So we'll have all day. We'd better not tell anyone."

"All right," said Agnes.

"Look!" said Agatha. "It's stopped raining. Let's go out and splash in the puddles."

Samantha followed the twins out of the shadowy attic, down the stairs, and into the bright, warm sunshine. She carried the sketchbook carefully in both hands. Now that she had found it, she never wanted to let it go.

CHAPTER THREE

TEARDROP ISLAND

Samantha and the twins set out early the next day. Their pack baskets were jammed with sandwiches and cookies, butterfly nets, bird guides, and magnifying glasses—the same equipment they started out with every morning. But this morning, Samantha had her mother's sketchbook tucked away under the picnic blanket in her pack basket.

The Admiral came down to the dock to help the girls push off. "Where are you off to today, mateys?" he asked.

"Just exploring," answered Agnes lightly.

"Well, keep an eye on the weather," warned the Admiral. "It could turn nasty. That storm could

269

twist around and hit us again
today. Anchors aweigh! Cheerio!"

"Cheerio!" the girls called
back as their canoe glided into the deeper water. It
was another hot day. The sun burned so strong, it
seemed to have bleached the sky white. "As soon
as we get to the island, I'm going straight to the
waterfall," announced Agnes. "It looks so cool in
the pictures."

"I'm climbing right up to that rocky cliff at the
end of the island," said Agatha. "I can't wait to see
the view."

"I want to see *everything*," said Samantha. She
wondered what Teardrop Island would be like.
Would it be just the way it was in her mother's
pictures? Would she remember being there with her
parents? Would it seem friendly and familiar, or
scary and strange?

The lake was flat and peaceful. The girls paddled
steadily, and soon Piney Point was out of sight.

"Watch it! Rocks ahead!" warned Agatha from
the front of the canoe. The lake was suddenly
narrow. Steep hills rose up on either side. Big
boulders stuck up out of the water. Jagged rocks hid

just below the surface. The water churned white where it splashed against the rocks.

The girls were quiet. They gripped their paddles and steered carefully. They had to zig and zag to find the best path around the sharp rocks.

"Go to the left!" Agatha would shout, and then, "Quick! To the right!" Samantha felt sweat from heat and fear dripping down her back. But the canoe was high in the water, so it slipped smoothly over the rocks beneath it. And it was so slender, it slithered between the boulders as easily as a fish.

Finally, they were through the narrow passage and into a wider, deeper part of the lake.

"Phew!" said Samantha.

"We did it!" cheered Agatha, waving her paddle over her head.

"I bet even the Admiral couldn't have done better," boasted Agnes.

Now the canoe seemed to float by itself across the water into the cool shadow of Teardrop Island. As they came near the island, the girls could hear a chorus of birds singing gaily, as if the island itself were welcoming them. They saw a small stretch of pebbly shore where they could land the canoe. The rest of the shore was made up of big rocks.

As soon as the water was shallow enough, Agatha hopped out of the canoe and pulled the front end out of the water and up onto the pebbly shore. Samantha and Agnes quickly gathered up their pack baskets and climbed out, too. They were so excited, they rushed up the steep shore and into the piney woods.

"We're here!" crowed Agnes. They threaded their way between the tall pine trees and moss-covered rocks. There seemed to be an old path, but it was so overgrown with giant ferns and long grass, it was hard to tell. Overhead, leaves fluttered hello and squirrels leaped from tree to tree, inspecting their visitors.

"It's like a jungle!" exclaimed Agatha as she batted a branch away. "Now we're really explorers."

"It looks like the enchanted forest in *Sleeping Beauty*," said Samantha. "It's as if it's been under a spell for a hundred years, just waiting for us to come."

The branches of the trees hung so low over the

path, it was like walking through a green tunnel. But once in a while, the girls would come into an open space between the trees where a surprise batch of wildflowers grew.

"I hear the waterfall!" cried Samantha. She ran ahead of the others to a sunny clearing. And there it was, looking just exactly the way it did in her mother's painting: a lacy curtain of water splashing down giant steps of stones. The water spray caught the sun and made little rainbows. Samantha's heart thudded. It was the most beautiful thing she had ever seen.

Without a word, the three girls pulled off their shoes and stockings. They bunched up their skirts and waded into the shallow pool at the foot of the waterfall. They got as close to the fall as they could and let the spray mist their faces. The water was icy cold. It felt wonderful after their hot canoe ride.

"Next time we come, we'll have to bring our bathing suits," said Agnes.

Samantha grinned. "I don't mind getting wet," she said. She pulled off her middy blouse and skirt and walked straight into the waterfall in her chemise and drawers. Agatha was right behind her.

*And there it was, looking just exactly the way it did
in her mother's painting.*

"Ooooh!" they shrieked with glee as the water showered them. "Come on in, Agnes! It's *freezing!*"

Agnes took off her blouse and skirt, folded them carefully, and began to walk slowly into the pool. Then, *oops!* She slipped on a mossy stone and fell, *plunk!*, on her bottom.

Samantha and Agatha laughed as they helped her stand up. "That's the fast way to get wet," Samantha giggled. She let the water pour down on her head and neck and shoulders until she couldn't stand the cold any longer. Then she ran out into the sunshine, and then back into the falls again.

After a while, the girls were cold down to their bones, so they stretched out on a warm rock to dry off. Samantha lay on her stomach and put her face into the water for a drink. "Oh!" she sputtered. "It's so cold, it makes my nose numb!"

Agnes nodded. "My skin is all tingly," she said. "And I'm hungry. Let's have our picnic."

They spread the picnic blanket on the rock and sat cross-legged, holding their big sandwiches in both hands.

"This is the nicest place I've ever been in my whole life," said Agatha.

"It's so peaceful," said Agnes. "All you can hear are water, birds, and the breeze."

"Now that you've seen the waterfall, do you remember coming here with your mother and father?" Agatha asked Samantha.

Samantha kicked one leg in the water, sending sparkling drops into the air. "I think so," she said slowly. "I feel as if I've been here before, but it's all mixed up. It's almost like dreaming."

"Well, it's a dreamy place," said Agnes. She tilted her face up to the sun. Water drops hung in her hair like pearls.

"I'm very glad your mother drew those pictures," said Agatha. "Otherwise we'd never have come here."

Samantha looked around. It gave her goose bumps to think that she was in a place she had been with her mother and father, and that nothing had changed. This very same rock and those very same trees were all in the pictures her mother had painted.

"Come on!" said Samantha. She stood up and brushed the crumbs off her lap. "Let's get dressed and explore. I want to find all the places my mother drew." She took her mother's sketchbook out of her pack basket.

"All right," agreed the twins.

Family picnic, Summer 1897

The sketchbook was like a treasure map. It led the girls on a long, happy hunt. First they found the grassy field where Samantha and her parents used to have picnics. It was just as sunny as it looked in the picture Samantha's mother had painted.

The girls looked a long time before they found the big split rock that was in another picture. They found flowers growing in the shade of graceful white birch trees. The same flowers were in the picture that showed Samantha and her father picking a bouquet.

And finally, the girls climbed up to the highest point of the island so they could see the view. The dark green pines and the hills that sloped down to the wide lake looked the same as they did in the pictures Samantha's mother had painted.

Picking flowers with Father

"Gosh! You can touch the
clouds up here!" said Agatha.

"Look, there's the goose's
neck," said Agnes. She pointed to the narrow
rocky part of the lake they had paddled through
that morning.

"And there's Piney Point," said Samantha. "It
looks very small from here."

The girls were so high up, they seemed to be
standing where the sky met the land. The wind
tugged at Samantha's skirt as if it wanted to lift her
up like a kite into the clouds.

Samantha looked at the sky. The clouds were
dark and heavy. "I think we'd better go," she said
to the twins. "It looks like it might rain."

Agatha squinted up at the clouds. "You're
right," she said with a sigh. "But I hate to leave."

"We can come back," said Agnes.

"Oh yes," agreed Samantha. "We can always
come back, anytime we want to."

They hiked back to the waterfall, gathered up
their belongings, and put their pack baskets on
their backs. Samantha felt tired but content as they
walked down the narrow path to the lake shore.

What a glorious day! She would remember it forever and ever. She was very glad they had come.

As the girls came to the edge of the water, the leaves of the silver maples were showing their shiny undersides. That was always a sign that a storm was coming.

"Is this where we left the canoe?" asked Agatha.

"I think so," said Samantha.

"Well, I don't see it," said Agatha.

"Uh oh," said Agnes. The girls stood in a row on the pebbly shore.

"Didn't you tie it up?" Agatha asked Agnes.

"No!" Agnes wailed. "I thought you did."

"Well," said Samantha calmly, "it's probably just drifted off a little bit. Let's walk around the shore and see if it's washed up somewhere else."

It was very hard to walk around the shore of the island. The girls had to climb up and down big jagged rocks that were slippery from the lake spray. Soon all three girls were wet and out of breath. The canoe was nowhere in sight.

"I'm cold," complained Agnes. "What will we do now?"

"Swim home?" Agatha suggested desperately.

Samantha wished she could laugh, but Agatha's silly ideas didn't seem very funny now. "We have to use our heads," she said. "Let's go back up to the rocky cliff. We can see all around the island from up there. We're sure to spot the canoe."

Wearily, they trudged up the same hill that they'd scampered up just a few hours earlier. They followed the path past the waterfall and up to the rocky cliff. By now the sky was the color of tarnished silver and the wind was strong. Samantha held her wet hair in one hand to keep it from blowing in her face. She looked all around, but there was no canoe to be seen. No canoe at all. Samantha's stomach flopped with fear.

"We're stranded!" moaned Agatha. "How will we ever get back to Piney Point?"

"Someone will come and get us," said Samantha.

"But how will they know we're here?" asked Agnes.

"We could send smoke signals," said Agatha.

"But we don't have matches. How can we start a fire?" asked Samantha.

"Uh, you rub two sticks together, I think,"

said Agatha, uncertainly. "Or you can make paper catch fire with a magnifying glass. I read that in a book!" She pawed through her pack basket and dragged out her magnifying glass.

"It won't work. The sun's got to be shining," Samantha said. And the sun certainly was not shining at the moment. Big black clouds crowded next to each other, blocking the sun completely.

"Maybe if we made lots of noise, someone would hear us," said Agnes.

So Samantha blew on her bo's'n's whistle as hard as she could. Agnes and Agatha shouted, "Help! Help! Somebody help!" But the wind was blowing so hard, they knew no one could hear them. They gave up and looked longingly toward home.

"Jeepers, I'm hungry," said Agatha. "It must be dinnertime by now."

"Well, at least, when we're not home for dinner, they'll realize something is wrong," said Agnes. "In fact, they probably started looking for us when we weren't back to swim with the Admiral."

Samantha hoped Agnes was right. She sat down

next to a big rock to get shelter from the wind. It was getting colder and colder. All three girls wrapped up together in the picnic blanket, but it didn't help much. It felt as if they sat there for hours, watching the sky get darker and darker. A chilling drizzle began to fall.

"We may have to sleep here tonight," said Agatha, hugging her knees to her chest.

Agnes shuddered. "I hope there are no wild animals to creep up on us."

Samantha started to say, "No, I don't think—" when they heard a rustling sound below them on the path.

"What's *that?*" Agatha cried.

"Shh!" hissed Agnes.

The girls heard more rustling. It might have been the wind, but it sounded more like a bear or a wolf, pushing through the trees, coming closer and closer. Then they heard a moan!

Samantha gasped.

"Eeek!" yelped Agnes. She clutched Samantha's arm. The girls held their breath and listened. The sounds came closer: another moan, more rustling, then a crash.

Samantha grabbed a big stick and stood up. "Get behind me," she whispered to Agnes and Agatha.

They heard the moan once more, and then a low voice struggling to be heard over the wind. "Help! Help me!"

Samantha lowered the stick. "Who's there?" she called.

"Help!" the voice called again. "Oh! Samantha, help!"

The girls looked at each other, then started toward the voice, stumbling over one another as they headed down the hill. There, lying across the muddy path, was the Admiral!

"Admiral!" cried Samantha. She hurried toward him and knelt by his side. "What happened?"

The Admiral's voice was weak. "My head, my head . . ." he gasped. "I fell and hit it on the . . . on the . . . rocks." He put his hand up to his eye. In the darkness and rain, Samantha could just barely see the deep gash on his forehead and the blood that was trickling from it. The Admiral's eyelids drooped and he moaned again. "I came to . . . to help you," he whispered. "But now you'll have to help me." He tried to go on, but his voice failed, his eyes closed, and his head dropped onto the ground.

THROUGH THE
PASSAGE

"Is he dead?" asked Agatha hoarsely.

"No!" said Samantha. "I think he's unconscious." The Admiral's eyes were still closed.

"What will we do now?" wailed Agnes.

Samantha didn't want the twins to see how afraid she really was. She tried to act as if she knew just what to do. "Well," she said, "the first thing we have to do is to make him comfortable. Let's get him over to that rock where we ate lunch. The trees will give us a little shelter from the rain. We'll have to drag him."

Agnes took one of the Admiral's arms, and Samantha took the other. Very slowly, pulling with all their strength, the girls moved the Admiral over to the flat rock by the pool. The Admiral groaned, but he did not open his eyes.

"He needs a doctor," said Samantha. "We've got to get him back to Piney Point as fast as we can."

"But how can we even get him to his boat?" asked Agnes. "He's too heavy to carry or drag all that way."

"We'll have to help him walk," said Samantha. She put her cold hand on the Admiral's forehead, then she shook his shoulder. "Admiral? Admiral, can you hear me?"

Slowly, he opened his eyes. Samantha and the twins gently helped him sit up. Then Samantha put one of his arms over her shoulder. Agnes took his other arm, and together they lifted him so that he was standing. He swayed for a moment, but then he steadied himself.

"Lean on us, Admiral," said Samantha. "We're going down to the boat."

The Admiral didn't say anything, but Samantha heard him take a deep breath. He tried to stand up straighter. His arm was heavy on Samantha's shoulder. Agatha gathered up all the pack baskets and led the way down to the shore. Agnes and Samantha struggled behind her, holding on to the Admiral's waist to steady him. The narrow path was slippery now because of the rain. Agnes and Samantha had to push wet branches out of the way with their free hands.

"That's it, that's good," Samantha murmured with every step. "You're doing fine, Admiral. Not much farther now."

The Admiral had left a lighted lantern in his boat. They headed toward it in the darkness. When they finally reached the boat, they helped the Admiral swing his legs over the side and lie down on the bottom. Samantha took a napkin from her pack basket, dipped it in the cold lake water, and laid it gently over the bloody cut on the Admiral's forehead. The girls covered him with their picnic blanket to help keep him warm.

"Girls . . ." the Admiral began. But his voice trailed off to nothing, and he closed his eyes again.

"All right," said Agatha in a wavery voice. "Let's go."

The three girls shoved the heavy rowboat into the water. The twins jumped in and sat side by side on the middle seat, each one taking an oar. Samantha knelt in the front, holding the lantern to light the way through the rain.

The Admiral's boat was much bigger and harder to handle than the canoe. The twins had to struggle against the wind and the choppy waves that slapped the sides of the boat. But they rowed slowly and steadily until they came to the narrow part of the lake where the rocks broke through the water.

"It's too narrow to row in here!" exclaimed Agatha.

"Use your oars to push off from the rocks," shouted Samantha.

The bottom of the heavy old boat scraped against rocks that were hiding beneath the water. On either side, boulders poked up out of the water like dark monsters. "Push right!" cried Samantha, then, "Right again. Hard!"

The boat rocked wildly from side to side, knocking against the boulders. Water splashed into the girls' faces and drenched their clothes.

"It was probably like this the night my parents drowned,"
Samantha said to herself.

It was probably like this the night my parents drowned, Samantha said to herself. She shivered. Behind her, the Admiral stirred and groaned. *We've got to get through this passage,* Samantha thought. *We've got to get the Admiral back to Piney Point as soon as we can.*

Suddenly, the boat stopped with a hard *thud.* "We're stuck!" Agnes wailed. The front of the boat was caught between two big rocks. Samantha stood up and pushed against one of the rocks to get the boat free. She pushed so hard, she lost her balance and almost toppled out into the water. She steadied herself and pushed again, and finally the boat was free.

"Quick! Everybody push hard to the left," Samantha yelled. After one more push they were out of the narrow passage, headed into the wide, black lake.

They had no time to catch their breath. The twins began to row again. They hunched over the oars, trying to keep the rain out of their eyes. They rowed as hard as they could, on and on, through the stormy darkness, across the lake that seemed as huge and endless as the ocean.

"Lights!" Samantha shouted at last. "I see lights! It's Piney Point!"

The twins twisted around to look at the welcome sight. In the main house at Piney Point, every lamp was lit. There were lights on the dock, and lights were bobbing in boats on the water.

"Grandmary! Uncle Gard!" Samantha yelled. "Help!" She waved the lantern back and forth and blew on her bo's'n's whistle again and again and again. Some of the lights seemed to be coming closer.

"I think they see us!" she called to the twins over her shoulder. "I think they're coming!" She waved the lantern over her head. "Over here! Over here!" she shouted.

Out of the dark, she heard Uncle Gard call, "Samantha!" And suddenly, there he was in another boat alongside of them. "Samantha!" he said again. "Catch this rope. Tie it to the front of your boat. I'm going to haul you in."

"Hurry, Uncle Gard," Samantha said. "We've got the Admiral

with us. He's hurt."

Uncle Gard tossed a heavy, wet rope to Samantha. She tied it to the front of the rowboat as well as she could. "All right," she called.

With a jolt and a thump, Uncle Gard's boat began to pull them toward Piney Point. The boats moved quickly, and in no time they were at the dock. In the jumble of voices and lights, Samantha didn't even know who lifted her out of the rowboat.

"Be careful!" she said as the men began to move the Admiral. "He's hurt. Watch his head." And then Grandmary was hugging her so hard, she could barely breathe.

"Oh my dear," murmured Grandmary. She smoothed Samantha's hair away from her face. "Oh my dear. Thank God you're all right."

Together, Grandmary and Samantha climbed the steps up the hill. Samantha's legs were wobbly. She leaned against Grandmary and followed the path of lights to the main house. At last, she and the twins and the Admiral were all safe.

Later on, the three girls were sitting in front of the fire in the big room of the main house. Cornelia had given them all hot baths, rubbed them dry, and wrapped them in blankets. They sat quietly, sipping their cocoa,,watching the doctor take care of the Admiral.

"You're a lucky fellow, Admiral," said the doctor. He wrapped a clean white bandage around the Admiral's forehead. "It's a good thing these girls got you home so quickly. This cut could have been very serious. How did it happen?"

"Well," said the Admiral, "when I saw the storm coming up, I set out to find the girls. They weren't on the lake nearby, so I knew they'd gone through the passage. I had a bit of a time getting past those rocks in the rowboat—"

"Oh, the rocks in that passage are terrible!" said Grandmary. "Especially in a storm!" Her face was pale.

The Admiral squeezed her hand to comfort her, then went on. "Once I was through, I heard your whistle, Samantha. Then I saw your canoe. It was partly sunk in the water near Teardrop Island.

I suppose you didn't beach it properly."

The girls hung their heads.

"I realized you were stranded on the island, so I hurried to help you. I landed my boat and jumped out, but I slipped on the rocks and hit my head. After that, I don't remember much. I think I tried to find you. The next thing I knew, you were helping me into the boat. And then we were home, safe and sound at Piney Point."

The Admiral sat up in his chair as if it were a throne and his bandage were a crown. "I'm proud to know you girls," he said. He patted Samantha on the hand. "You really saved the day, young lady."

Grandmary sighed. "I was so worried about you, *all* of you," she said. "I was so afraid. It was just like the night, that awful night . . ." She shook her head.

Samantha had never seen her grandmother look so weary. "I'm sorry we frightened you, Grandmary," she said. "I didn't mean to. I just had to go to Teardrop Island. I had to see the waterfall."

"You remembered the waterfall?" Grandmary

The Admiral patted Samantha on the hand.
"You really saved the day, young lady."

asked. She looked surprised.

"No," answered Samantha. "I didn't remember it. I saw it in this book." She pulled the sketchbook out from the folds of her blanket.

"Lydia's sketchbook," said Uncle Gard softly. "I haven't seen that in years. Not since . . ." He didn't finish his sentence.

Samantha handed the book to Grandmary. "I didn't remember anything about Teardrop Island. I didn't know I had ever been there with my parents, until I saw this book," she said. "That's why I had to go there today. I wanted to see the waterfall and all the places on the island we used to go. I wanted to try to remember what it was like when we all went there together, as a family."

Grandmary stared down at the book in her lap. "You and your parents had many happy times on that island," she said. "You are right to try to remember."

"It all looks exactly the same, Grandmary," Samantha said. "Everything on the island is just as pretty as it is in my mother's drawings. It's a beautiful, happy place. I'd like to go back again." She looked up at Grandmary. "Maybe you'd like to come with me sometime."

"Perhaps I will," Grandmary said softly.
"Perhaps I will."

TO THE PETTY, HEUER, AND
DALTON FAMILIES

CHANGES FOR
Samantha

BY VALERIE TRIPP

CHAPTER
ONE

A NEW HOME

Samantha hurried along the city sidewalk with her ice skates slung over one shoulder. Oh, it was cold! She pulled her hat down over her ears and then rubbed her hands together inside her snug fur muff. The wintry afternoon sky was pink darkening to purple as she ran up the steps to Uncle Gard and Aunt Cornelia's house. "Hello!" she called out as she pushed open the heavy door and came into the bright hallway. "I'm home!"

"There you are, dear!" said Aunt Cornelia. She gave Samantha a hug. "I was afraid you'd frozen to the ice! It must have been awfully cold at the skating pond this afternoon. Come sit by the fire and have some tea. That will warm you up."

Samantha followed Aunt Cornelia into the cozy parlor. She sat by the fire and held her stiff hands up to the glow to melt the coldness away. This was Samantha's favorite time of the day now that she lived in New York City with Uncle Gard and Aunt Cornelia. Every afternoon as dusk settled over the city, Samantha and Aunt Cornelia shared a pot of tea and chatted while they waited for Uncle Gard to come home from his office. This afternoon, Samantha noticed a big box on the tea table. A bit of silky pink ribbon was slipping out from under the lid. "What's in the box, Aunt Cornelia?" she asked.

"Valentines!" said Aunt Cornelia. She lifted the lid and turned the box upside down. Out spilled loops of ribbon, paper lace doilies, tiny red hearts, and sheets of paper covered with pictures of cupids and flowers. "Saint Valentine's Day is only a few weeks away. I thought we'd better start making our valentines now, since—"

"We have so many to make this year!" Samantha finished eagerly. She picked up a pink ribbon and two hearts. "My first valentine will be for Grandmary and the Admiral."

"The newly-weds!" smiled Aunt Cornelia.

"I'll make two hearts joined together," said Samantha. "That seems right for people who just got married, doesn't it?"

"Yes, indeed!" said Aunt Cornelia. She began cutting out pictures of cupids.

"Oh, it's so romantic," sighed Samantha. "I mean the way Grandmary and the Admiral finally got married after being so fond of each other for all those years."

"Mmm," agreed Aunt Cornelia.

"I'm sure they're happy, sailing around the world on the Admiral's yacht," said Samantha. "I do miss them both just terribly. But I'm glad I live here with you and Uncle Gard."

"We're glad, too!" smiled Aunt Cornelia.

Just then the parlor door opened. "Begging your pardon, madam," a cool voice interrupted. It was Gertrude, the housekeeper. She was carrying the tea tray. Samantha sat up a little straighter. Gertrude always made her feel as if she had done something wrong. Now Gertrude looked down her long nose

at the messy tea table covered with bits of ribbon
and paper. "And *where* shall I place the tray,
madam?" she asked Aunt Cornelia.

"Oh, anywhere will do," said Aunt Cornelia.
She didn't look up. She was busy pasting cupids
onto paper lace doilies.

Gertrude didn't move.

"Just put it on Samantha's stool by the fire,
Gertrude," said Aunt Cornelia. "Sam can sit on the
floor."

"The *floor*, madam?" sniffed Gertrude.

"Yes," said Aunt Cornelia. "And Gertrude,
would you mix up another batch of flour paste for
us, please? We've used up this jar." She handed
Gertrude the sticky jar of paste.

If Aunt Cornelia had handed her a pail of
snakes and hoptoads, Gertrude could not have
looked more disgusted. She held the paste jar with
the very tips of her fingers as she left the room.

Aunt Cornelia brought Samantha a cup of
sweet, hot tea and looked down at the valentine
Samantha had just finished. "Oh, how
lovely!" she exclaimed. "Grandmary
and the Admiral will love it!"

"Oh, how lovely!" Aunt Cornelia exclaimed.
"Grandmary and the Admiral will love it!"

Samantha set the valentine carefully on a corner of the table. "Now I'll make one for Nellie," she said. "This one really has to be especially pretty because Nellie is my very best friend in Mount Bedford."

"You miss her a lot, don't you?" said Aunt Cornelia.

"Yes," said Samantha. "And I worry about her, too. She has to work very hard at Mrs. Van Sicklen's, and she's not very strong."

Aunt Cornelia sighed. "But Nellie is better off there than she would be here in the city."

"I know," said Samantha. "When Nellie lived in the city before, she worked in a terrible, dangerous factory. It was horrible."

"At least Nellie had a loving family to go home to," said Aunt Cornelia. "Lots of children who work in those factories are orphans. The lucky ones live in orphanages. The others live on the streets."

Samantha shivered. She had seen many poor, raggedy children in the city. She was glad Nellie was safe with her family in Mount Bedford, even if she *was* far away. "Maybe we could make valentine cookies and send them to Nellie," said Samantha.

"What a good idea!" said Aunt Cornelia. "We'll make cookies for Nellie and Agnes and Agatha . . ."

"And Uncle Gard!" added Samantha. "It will be a surprise for him!"

"A surprise?" Uncle Gard poked just his head into the parlor. "Are my two best girls planning a surprise for me? Well, I've got a surprise, too," he said. He reached into the pocket of his coat and handed Samantha a postcard and a letter.

"Oooh, look!" said Samantha. "It's a postcard from Grandmary and the Admiral." She read aloud Grandmary's elegant, spidery script:

My dear Samantha,

The Admiral and I are sailing in the warm, blue-green waters off Greece! It's lovely! We're very happy, but we do miss our dear girl. Please give our love to your Uncle Gardner and Aunt Cornelia!

Ever your devoted

Grandmary

Ahoy matey! xoxo
What ho! your
Admiral

307

Samantha laughed. "Look," she said. "The Admiral drew a picture for all of us." She handed the card to Uncle Gard and Aunt Cornelia and looked down at the letter in her lap. "Jiminy!" she exclaimed. "It's from Nellie!" She ripped open the envelope eagerly and began to read aloud.

> "Dear Samantha, How are you? I hope you are very happy living at your aunt and uncle's house. I am fine, but . . ."

Suddenly, Samantha stopped reading aloud because the words were too horrible. She read to herself:

I am fine, but I have some very sad news. The flu has been very bad here in Mount Bedford this winter. We all had it except Jenny. My mother and father died. I miss them so much. Mrs. Van Sicklen says they are in heaven where God will take care of them. Mrs. Van Sicklen has been kind, but now we must leave her house. Bridget and Jenny and I are moving to New York City to live with our Uncle Mike. I will come to see you as soon as I can. I promise.

Your friend,

Nellie

"Oh, poor Nellie!" Samantha whispered. "Poor Bridget and Jenny!"

"What is it, Samantha?" Aunt Cornelia asked.

Samantha couldn't talk. She was too afraid she would cry. She handed the letter to Aunt Cornelia.

Aunt Cornelia and Uncle Gard read it together. When they finished, Uncle Gard picked Samantha up and held her on his lap. Aunt Cornelia took both her hands.

"Sometimes," Aunt Cornelia said in a soft, slow voice, "sometimes it's very hard to understand why such sad, sad things happen to good people, people we love. Nellie and her sisters are very young to be without their parents. But they have their uncle, and I am sure he will take care of them."

Uncle Gard cleared his throat. Samantha knew

he and Aunt Cornelia were both just as sad as she
was. "Nellie and her little sisters will be in New
York, Sam. They won't be far away anymore," he
said. "We'll be able to see them and be sure they're
all right. Isn't that so, Cornelia?"

Aunt Cornelia didn't answer, but she squeezed
Samantha's hands.

"Nellie says she'll come to see me when she
gets to New York," Samantha said. It was the one
good thing in the middle of the sadness—like one
candle in a big, dark room. "Nellie promised to
come, so I know she will. Oh, I hope she comes
soon!"

C H A P T E R
T W O
—

SEARCHING FOR NELLIE

Days and days went by, but Nellie never came. There was no note, no message, no word at all from her. Every afternoon Samantha hurried home from school and sat, waiting, in the front parlor. She pretended to do her schoolwork, but really she stared out the window, hoping to see Nellie coming toward her. But she saw only strangers.

Her hopes faded as each bright afternoon faded into gray twilight. She read Nellie's letter over and over again, adding up the days in her head. One day for Nellie to pack, one day to travel, one day with her uncle . . .

Samantha began to worry. Maybe something

311

had happened. Maybe Nellie was sick with the flu again. Maybe Mrs. Van Sicklen wanted her to stay in Mount Bedford. Or maybe her uncle wouldn't let her come to visit. Something had to be wrong, because if Nellie was in New York, Samantha knew that she would keep her promise.

The first few evenings, as soon as Uncle Gard came in the door, he asked about Nellie. "Did she come today, Sam?" But after a while, he didn't need to ask. He could tell the answer was no by the disappointed look on Samantha's face.

One night after dinner, Uncle Gard said, "Tonight we'll telephone Mrs. Van Sicklen and find out where Nellie and her sisters are."

"That's a good idea," said Aunt Cornelia.

"Telephone?" asked Samantha. "But it's all the way to Mount Bedford. That's long distance."

"Well, what else do we have a newfangled contraption like the telephone for?" asked Uncle Gard.

Samantha and Aunt Cornelia followed Uncle Gard into the hall-way and watched as he cranked the telephone. "Operator?" he shouted into the mouthpiece.

"Hello? Operator? I want to speak to the Van
Sicklen residence in Mount Bedford, please."
Samantha heard some loud crackling on the line,
and then Uncle Gard shouted, "Mrs. Van Sicklen,
please. Mrs. Van Sicklen? Gardner Edwards here.
No, no, nothing's wrong. Sorry to alarm you by
telephoning. We're wondering where Nellie is.
Nellie, your little maid, and her sisters Bridget
and Jenny."

Uncle Gard paused. Then his voice was serious.
"Two weeks ago? I see. Well, do you happen to
know their uncle's exact address? No? I don't
suppose he has a telephone? No, no, I thought not.
Well, thank you, Mrs. Van Sicklen. I'll ring off
now." He turned the crank, hung up the earpiece,
and looked at Samantha.

"Mrs. Van Sicklen says the girls left Mount
Bedford two weeks ago. She put them on the train
herself. The uncle's name is Mike O'Malley. Mrs.
Van Sicklen didn't know his exact address, but she
thinks he lives somewhere near the river, on 17th
or 18th Street."

"They left Mount Bedford two weeks ago,"
repeated Samantha. "Why hasn't Nellie come to see

me in all that time?"

"Nellie may be working," Uncle Gard said. "Or maybe she's too busy looking after Bridget and Jenny."

Samantha felt desperate. "Can't we try to find them? If we could just find where Nellie's uncle lives—"

"Samantha," Aunt Cornelia interrupted gently, "New York is a big place. It would be very hard— probably impossible—to find Nellie's uncle by just wandering around. I'm afraid all we can do is wait for Nellie to come to us."

"Don't give up hope, Sam," said Uncle Gard. "Nellie will come one of these days. I'm sure she will."

He tried to turn his worried frown into a smile, but Samantha could tell by his voice that Uncle Gard wasn't really sure Nellie *would* come. Samantha was quiet for a moment. She was thinking hard. Then she said, "Thank you for telephoning, Uncle Gard." She climbed up the stairs to her room. With each step, she was more determined. She didn't care how hard it would be. She was going to find Nellie. And she would go the very next day.

After school the next afternoon, Samantha set out under a heavy gray sky. She was more than a little nervous. In just a few blocks, she was in a part of the city she had never seen before. But she followed the street signs carefully and found 17th Street without any trouble. A strong wind at her back seemed to push her right to it.

But after she had walked toward the river for five or six blocks, 17th Street changed. Samantha had to jostle her way down the icy, muddy middle of the street because the sidewalks were blocked with pushcarts. The carts were piled high with potatoes, baskets, brooms, and buckets. The air was so full of the smell of fish and smoke, it seemed as dense as fog.

And there were so many people! Women dressed all in black with shawls over their heads poked at the things on the carts. Silent men stood next to small fires, rubbing their hands. Packs of raggedy-looking boys ran through the crowd.

Samantha began to feel as small and timid as a mouse in the hubbub around her. All the noise and strangeness was frightening. But she could not turn back. *It's a good thing there are so many people out on the street,* she said to herself bravely. *Someone here must know Nellie's uncle.*

But the cold that was chilling her hands and feet seemed to be freezing up her courage, too. When she saw steam rising from a cart of roasted chestnuts, she decided to get some because they looked so nice and hot.

Samantha handed the chestnut man a penny. As he gave her the bag of nuts, he said, "There you are, missy. The chestnuts will cheer ye. Put 'em in your muff to warm up your hands."

His singsong accent reminded Samantha of the way Nellie's father had talked. "Please, sir," she said. "Do you know Mr. O'Malley?"

The man grinned. "Sure and there are many, many O'Malleys, miss. Which one would you be wanting?"

"Mr. Mike O'Malley," said Samantha. "He lives on 17th or 18th Street."

The grin vanished from the man's face like a light blown out by a cold wind. "And what would a young missy such as yourself be wanting with a

hooligan like Mike O'Malley?" he asked.

"My friend Nellie, his niece, is with him," said Samantha. "Please, do you know where he lives?"

The man thought for a moment, then said, "Last I heard he was living—if you can call it that—over on 18th Street, above the shoemaker."

"Thank you!" said Samantha.

"Mind you be careful!" warned the chestnut man as Samantha hurried away.

She walked fast, but she was worried. Was Nellie's uncle a bad man? The chestnut man had called him a hooligan. Samantha was not sure what a hooligan was, but she was quite sure she did not want to meet one. Only the idea of finally seeing Nellie kept her going. By now she was expert at dodging people and carts. In no time she'd rounded the corner and found the shoemaker's shop on 18th Street. There, outside the shop, she stopped. She stood silently staring at the building.

Is this where Nellie lives? she wondered. The building was gloomy and horrible. It was falling apart and looked as if it were too tired to stand up anymore. Tattered laundry hung from the windows like grimy flags of defeat.

Samantha did not want to go in the dark doorway. Then she thought, *Maybe Nellie has to go in this doorway every single day. Maybe Nellie is inside there right now.*

She climbed the steps and went inside. The door slammed shut behind her as if the building were swallowing her whole. The hallway smelled like rotting garbage. It was so dark, Samantha could hardly see. She held her breath and started up the creaky steps. Suddenly, at the top of the steps, a door flew open and a woman stuck her head out.

"What do you want?" she asked in a hard voice.

Samantha froze. "I'm . . . uh, I'm looking for Mr. Mike O'Malley," she croaked.

"Hist!" frowned the woman. "You'll not find him here, I'm happy to say. Now go away!" She started to close the door.

"Please, ma'am," said Samantha. "I was told he lived here. I've got to find him. He's got Nellie, and . . ."

"Nellie?" asked the woman. She stopped closing the door. A little face appeared at her knees, peeking around her skirts, smiling at Samantha. The woman scooped up the baby and opened the door a bit wider. "Is it Nellie you're looking for?"

"Yes!" said Samantha.

The woman still didn't smile, but she said, "Come along in then! Quickly now!"

Samantha stepped inside. She stood awkwardly near the door in a small room. It was not much lighter than the hallway, but it was scrubbed clean. It was more crowded than any room Samantha had ever seen. It was everything at once. One part was a kitchen. There were beds, and chairs pushed together to make beds, in each corner. In the middle

of the room there was a wooden table where
six children sat. They were making flowers out
of paper. They all looked up shyly at Samantha,
but their fingers never stopped twisting the
colorful paper onto wire stems. It seemed odd
to see the bright blossoms in the middle of the
dark, cheerless room.

"All right, children," said the woman kindly.
"Gawking won't get the work done faster, will it?"
She bounced the baby on her hip while she told
her story. "That Mike O'Malley," she said, as if the
name were a curse. "He did live here, and drinking
was all he was good for, you'll pardon me saying,
miss. Then about two weeks ago, the three girls
came to live with him. Good, polite girls they were,
too. And if Mike O'Malley didn't take all of their
money, and anything else they had, and run off! He
left them all alone in that room upstairs. They had
nothing to eat and nowhere to sleep but the bare
floor. Well! The oldest one, that Nellie, was as
bright a child as I've ever seen. She tried to clean
up the place and make it decent, but they couldn't
stay there with no coal for a fire and not two
pennies to rub together. So I took them in here.

"But we're crowded in here already, as you can see," the woman said.
"So I had to take Nellie and her sisters to the orphanage."

They sat down to work, and there was never a word of complaint from one of them. But we're crowded in here already, as you can see. After about a week, Nellie said they couldn't stay and be eating our food any longer. So I did the only thing I knew to do. I took them to the orphanage, where at least they'll be safe and warm and fed and get some schooling. Aye, and didn't it break my heart to see them go."

"They're gone?" asked Samantha. "To an orphanage?"

"Yes," said the woman. "Over on 20th Street. It's called Coldrock House for Homeless Girls." She shook her head. "They've got no one left in the world to care for them now, poor things. Though you mark my words, they're better off without that good-for-nothing uncle."

Samantha couldn't believe what she had heard. Nellie and the girls were in an orphanage! Coldrock House didn't sound very warm or welcoming, but it had to be better than living with their Uncle Mike. "Thank you," Samantha said to the woman. "Now I know where to find Nellie. Thank you for being so kind."

"It's the least I could do for the dear girls," said the woman. "If you see Nellie and the little ones, give them my best love and say I still think of them and wish I could do more for them myself."

Samantha shook the woman's hand. "I will," she said. "I'll tell them."

Then she turned and rushed down the steps, out into the steely gray dusk. She hurried home through the shadowy streets, thinking only of Nellie and her sisters.

COLDROCK HOUSE

Samantha couldn't sleep that night. She pulled the blankets up to her nose, but above them her eyes were wide open. She listened to the swoosh and sigh of the sleet against her window. She heard the passing horses snort and stamp and jingle their harnesses to shake off the dreary cold. Mostly, she worried about Nellie. What kind of place was Coldrock House for Homeless Girls? Was Nellie all right there? Tomorrow she would see for herself.

The next morning at breakfast, Aunt Cornelia said, "You look tired, Samantha. Do you feel all right?"

"Oh yes, I'm fine," said Samantha. "I just . . .

324

I just didn't sleep too much last night."

Uncle Gard's face wrinkled with concern. "Now, Sam," he said, "I know you're worried about Nellie and the little ones. I am, too. It's hard not really knowing how they are, or even exactly where they are."

"I do know exactly where they are," Samantha said quietly.

"You do?" asked Uncle Gard and Aunt Cornelia together.

Samantha nodded. "Nellie and Bridget and Jenny are in an orphanage. It's called Coldrock House for Homeless Girls. It's on 20th Street."

Uncle Gard and Aunt Cornelia were silent.

"I know because I went to Nellie's uncle's house yesterday," Samantha went on. "And a neighbor told me about Nellie."

Uncle Gard and Aunt Cornelia looked at each other. Then Uncle Gard said, "Samantha, you went to a dangerous part of the city. Don't go there again. Do you understand?"

"Yes," said Samantha. "I'm sorry. I just had to try to find Nellie and the girls. And now I know where they are. At Coldrock House."

"I'll go to Coldrock House with you this afternoon," said Aunt Cornelia. "They might not allow you in if you're by yourself."

"Thank you!" said Samantha. She smiled for the first time that morning.

Aunt Cornelia smiled back. "We'll

valise

pack a small valise for Nellie and her sisters," she said. "I'm sure they could use some warm clothes."

"Yes! And books," said Samantha. "Nellie loves books, and pens and paper and . . ."

"Cookies!" exclaimed Uncle Gard. "And sweets!"

Samantha laughed. "You're right, Uncle Gard," she said as she hugged him. She knew he was relieved to know where Nellie and her sisters were, too.

It was biting cold that afternoon when Samantha and Aunt Cornelia walked to Coldrock House. Samantha followed her aunt up the steps to the stern, unwelcoming building. The building looked as if it had been built out of blocks of dirty gray ice. It was surrounded by a fence of sharp black spikes. Samantha couldn't tell if the spikes were meant to keep visitors *out* or the orphans *in*.

A pale, pinched-looking maid opened the door when Aunt Cornelia knocked. "Would you announce me to the directress?" Aunt Cornelia said. "I'm Cornelia Edwards, and this is my niece, Samantha Parkington."

Without a word, the maid led them to a dark, cold parlor. It was very, very quiet. Samantha couldn't believe the building had children in it. Didn't any of them make a noise?

Suddenly, soundlessly, a stout woman appeared. She was frowning. When she saw Aunt Cornelia and Samantha, her eyes narrowed for a moment. She studied her two well-dressed guests, and then she smiled a fake smile. Her eyes widened with put-on delight. "How perfectly lovely," she exclaimed, holding her hand out to Aunt Cornelia. "Mrs. Edwards! Miss Parkington! How nice of you to visit us! I'm Tusnelda Frouchy, the directress here at Coldrock House. Please sit down. And how may I help you? Have you come to hire a maid or a serving girl?"

"Not today," replied Aunt Cornelia. "We've come to see Nellie O'Malley."

Miss Frouchy looked surprised. Her sickly-sweet

smile faltered for a moment, then spread itself wide again. "That's impossible," she said. "Our girls have visitors on Sunday afternoons only, from three to four o'clock. That's the rule. I'm sorry." She didn't sound sorry at all.

"This is a special case," Aunt Cornelia said firmly. "Nellie is a dear friend of my niece's. We haven't seen her in a long time. I'm sure you understand."

Miss Frouchy patted Samantha's cheek. Her puffy hands were soft but very, very cold. Samantha did not think she liked Miss Tusnelda Frouchy.

"I had no idea Nellie had such perfectly lovely friends," Miss Frouchy said. She turned to the maid and snapped, "Get her." While they waited, Miss Frouchy went on. "Nellie and her sisters are new here at Coldrock House, and of course, they're still a bit . . . a bit independent-minded, shall we say. But they'll adjust, I'm sure. Our girls quickly learn the rules here: Obedience. Order. Discipline—"

"Nellie!" cried Samantha. She jumped out of her chair and ran to hug her friend. "Nellie! I'm so glad to see you!"

"Samantha?" Nellie didn't seem to believe her eyes. "Oh, Samantha! You're here!" Nellie's face was full of joy.

"I was so worried when you didn't come to Uncle Gard and Aunt Cornelia's," said Samantha. "I even went to your uncle's house to find you and Bridget and Jenny."

"You didn't!" gasped Nellie. Her eyes were wide. "How did you ever—"

"Nellie!" Miss Frouchy interrupted. Her voice was very sharp.

Samantha felt Nellie stiffen. "Yes, Miss Frouchy," Nellie said.

"We haven't forgotten our manners, have we? Say 'how do you do' to Mrs. Edwards." Miss Frouchy turned to Aunt Cornelia. "You'll have to forgive her." She sighed. "Good manners are an important part of Coldrock House training, but these rough girls come to us without any idea of polite behavior at all." She held up her hands helplessly.

Now Samantha was sure she didn't like Miss Frouchy. Imagine calling Nellie rough! She could feel her face grow red with anger. But she bit her tongue as Nellie curtsied and murmured, "How do you do, Mrs. Edwards."

"Nellie," Aunt Cornelia said kindly, "we're so sorry about your parents—"

"Such a sad thing!" interrupted Miss Frouchy. She shook her head and pursed her lips, pretending to feel sympathy.

"Do you and Bridget and Jenny need anything?" Aunt Cornelia asked Nellie.

Before Nellie could answer, Miss Frouchy exclaimed, "Oh, nothing at all! They have warm clothes, good food, and a roof over their heads. They're learning how to make their way in the world as servants. But most important of all, they're learning to be grateful to their betters and to be obedient, hard-working girls." She turned to Nellie and asked, "Isn't that so, Nellie?"

"Yes, Miss Frouchy, ma'am," said Nellie, looking down at the floor.

Samantha studied Nellie while Miss Frouchy made a long speech about what a fine place the orphanage was. Nellie's hair was chopped short. Her drab brown dress was much too big. It was

"But most important of all, they're learning to be grateful to their betters. Isn't that so, Nellie?" Miss Frouchy said.

made out of scratchy material as rough as a potato sack. Nellie looked smaller and thinner than ever. Miss Frouchy said she was getting good food, but Samantha could see she definitely wasn't getting *enough* of it.

"Nellie," she said in a quiet voice, hoping Miss Frouchy wouldn't hear. "Look. We brought some things for you and Bridget and Jenny. We brought books and clothes and socks." Samantha began to unpack the valise. "We even brought some gingerbread, and—"

Suddenly, Miss Frouchy pounced like a tiger and snatched the things away. "I'll keep these for Nellie," she said. "We don't want the girls eating too much rich food. It's not good for them. And we don't want to spoil them with gifts. It makes them selfish. Isn't that right, Nellie?"

Nellie looked at Samantha helplessly.

"Isn't that right, Nellie?" Miss Frouchy hissed. Her green eyes were narrowed.

"Yes, Miss Frouchy, ma'am," Nellie answered in a whisper.

Samantha didn't know what to do. She couldn't

talk to Nellie with Miss Frouchy there. Luckily,
Aunt Cornelia understood. "Miss Frouchy," she
said, "would you be kind enough to give me a tour
of Coldrock House? I'm so interested in your work
here."

Miss Frouchy seemed to puff up with pleasure
and pride. "Why, of course," she said. "Do come
with me."

Aunt Cornelia smiled and winked at the girls
as she followed Miss Frouchy from the room.

"Jiminy! That Miss Frouchy is terrible!"
exclaimed Samantha when she and Nellie were
alone. "I just know she'll eat that gingerbread all
by herself."

Nellie grinned, and suddenly she looked like
her old self.

"Oh, Nellie," Samantha said. "Are you really,
really all right?"

"It's not so bad here," said Nellie. "At least
we're together. That's the most important thing of
all."

"Are Bridget and Jenny all right?" asked
Samantha.

Nellie's grin faded. "Well, Bridget's not strong,

and Miss Frouchy thinks she's lazy and scolds her terribly. I try to do Bridget's work for her, but it's hard to fool Miss Frouchy. She's everywhere! She's as sneaky as a cat."

Samantha squinted her eyes and made a catty face like Miss Frouchy's. "Perfectly lovely!" she mimicked.

Nellie tried to hide her giggles behind her hand.

Samantha sighed. "I wish you three could come to live with Uncle Gard and Aunt Cornelia and me," she said.

"No," said Nellie. "They've got all the maids they need. They don't want us."

"Well then, you could run away from here and *hide* at Uncle Gard and Aunt Cornelia's!" said Samantha. "They'd never know. You could stay in the attic, and I could take care of you and bring you food and everything—"

"Samantha," interrupted Nellie, "you know that would never work. If we ran away, we'd be caught and punished—really punished." Nellie looked very serious. "The best thing we can do is to stay here. They're training me to be a maid. Pretty soon they'll find a job for me, and I'll be able to work and take care of Bridget and Jenny."

"But—" Samantha began.

"Don't you see?" said Nellie. "All we've got is one another. Bridget and Jenny and I *have* to stay together. That's all that matters."

Samantha knew she could not change Nellie's mind. "Can you at least come visit Uncle Gard and Aunt Cornelia and me?"

"No," said Nellie. "Miss Frouchy wouldn't let us. But you can visit us here on Sundays."

"Only for an hour, and with that grouchy Miss Frouchy watching us," said Samantha. "Oh, well," she sighed. "It's better than nothing. And I can bring you things, lots of things, like—" Just then Miss Frouchy came back into the room, so the girls had to stop talking. She hardly let them say good-bye before she sent Nellie away.

Aunt Cornelia was very quiet on the walk home. Samantha could tell she had not liked what she had seen of Coldrock House. All she said was, "Those poor children." She shook her head and put her arm around Samantha's shoulder to hold her close by her side.

RUNAWAYS!

Uncle Gard, Aunt Cornelia, and
Samantha were waiting outside
Coldrock House at exactly five minutes
before three o'clock the next Sunday afternoon.
They didn't want to miss a second of their visiting
hour with Nellie, Bridget, and Jenny. They were all
quite cheerful when they arrived, but they left
feeling sad.

All the way home, Uncle Gard fussed and
fumed about the way Miss Frouchy treated the
girls. He had spent the hour talking to Bridget and
Jenny. He had kept a serious expression on his face,
hoping to fool Miss Frouchy into thinking he was
quizzing the girls on the multiplication tables. But

really he was asking them, "Miss Bridget O'Malley, where did you get those wonderful curls?" and "Miss Jenny O'Malley, how did you make your eyes such a pretty blue?" Bridget and Jenny tried to answer him just as seriously, but once in a while they'd break out into giggles. Whenever they did, they looked nervously at Miss Frouchy. She would narrow her eyes and frown at them. And when Uncle Gard tried to give them some sweets, Miss Frouchy grabbed them away.

Samantha and Nellie talked as much and as fast as they could, but one hour was nowhere near enough time. At the end of the visit, Samantha asked Nellie in a whisper, "Can't we meet secretly? What if I sneak over here in the middle of the night when everyone is asleep? I can tap on your window, and you can climb out."

Nellie laughed. "I have a better idea. What if you came in the afternoon, on your way home from school? It's my job to empty the ashes from the fireplaces. I bring them to the ash cans in the alley out back every afternoon about four o'clock. Could you come then?"

"Oh, of course!" said Samantha.

So every afternoon after school, Samantha hurried off to visit Nellie at Coldrock House. Samantha had to be very careful to get there by four o'clock. If she was even five minutes late, she didn't see Nellie at all.

Even though they met almost every afternoon, it never seemed that the girls had enough time together. While they talked, Samantha emptied the ashes into the cans so that Nellie had time to eat the food Samantha brought her. Nellie always looked hungry and tired and pale. Samantha noticed her friend's hands were red and chapped from the cold, so she gave Nellie her gloves. But the next afternoon, Nellie wasn't wearing them.

"Why aren't you wearing the gloves?" Samantha asked.

Nellie looked sorry. "Miss Frouchy took them," she said.

"That old cat!" exclaimed Samantha. "Didn't you tell her they were yours?"

"Yes," said Nellie, "but when I wouldn't tell her where I got them, she said I must have stolen them."

"Stolen them!" sputtered Samantha. "*She* stole

them from *you!* I'd like to march right inside and take those gloves away from Miss Tusnelda Frouchy."

"Samantha, don't," Nellie warned. "If Miss Frouchy knew we were meeting, she'd be awfully mad. She'd—"

"Punish you?" Samantha finished for her.

Nellie nodded.

"Did she punish you for the gloves?" Samantha asked.

Nellie nodded again. "No dinner," she said.

Samantha frowned. "From now on I'll bring more food instead of things like gloves. You can eat it right away or give it to Bridget and Jenny."

"That would be much better," said Nellie.

"I'll bring as much food as I can sneak past Gertrude," Samantha promised. "She's our stingy housekeeper. She's already noticed I seem to need more food than I ever did before. It won't be easy, so don't you let fat old Miss Frouchy get any of it!"

"Don't worry," grinned Nellie. "We'll eat it so fast, she'll never get a whiff of it!"

As the days went by, the afternoons seemed to be getting softer. The sun was still as pale as a pearl, but every day more light and warmth found its way to the narrow alley behind Coldrock House where Nellie and Samantha met. Then one afternoon, Nellie seemed much quieter than usual. She hardly seemed to hear Samantha's questions, and she put the apples Samantha brought in her apron pocket without even looking at them.

"What's the matter, Nellie?" Samantha asked at last. "Has Miss Frouchy been punishing you again?"

"No," said Nellie.

"Then what?" asked Samantha.

Nellie slammed the lid onto the ash can so loudly, it made Samantha jump. "They've picked me to go on the orphan train," said Nellie.

"What's *that*?" asked Samantha.

"It's a train that goes out West. It's full of orphans from the city. The train stops in lots of little farm towns. People in the towns choose orphans to live with them and to work for them," Nellie explained.

Samantha was horrified. "But Nellie, you *can't*

*"They've picked me to go out West
on the orphan train," said Nellie.*

leave New York!"

"I don't have any choice," Nellie said. "Miss Frouchy says I have to go. I'm trained enough now, and I'm old enough to work. Farm people might want me."

"What about Bridget and Jenny?" Samantha asked.

"They're too young to go," Nellie said softly. "They'll stay here."

"Oh, no," said Samantha. "You'll be separated."

"Yes," said Nellie. Her eyes filled with tears.

"Nellie, we can't let that happen," Samantha said. "You and Bridget and Jenny may never see one another again." She looked Nellie square in the eyes. "Now you've *got* to run away. You've *got* to come to Uncle Gard and Aunt Cornelia's house and hide. Just for a while, just until we think of something else to do. Please, Nellie, please say you'll come."

Nellie thought for a moment. "If I could look for work while I was there . . ."

"Oh, yes!" said Samantha. "You can go out every morning and come back in at night. No one will see you. I'll be sure of that. And I'll be sure you have food and blankets and everything you need."

Nellie sighed. "It's not a very practical plan," she said. "It won't work for long, but it's our only choice."

"Then you'll do it?" asked Samantha.

Nellie smiled a little smile. "I guess so," she said. "We might as well try."

Samantha hugged Nellie hard. "Good!" she said. "Bring Bridget and Jenny with you tomorrow afternoon at four."

"All right," said Nellie. "I'll find a way."

"Don't worry," said Samantha. "I'll plan everything. You'll see, Nellie. It will be fine. This will be your last night at Coldrock House."

"I hope so," said Nellie. "I certainly hope so."

The next day after school, Samantha ran to Coldrock House so fast, she was there way too early. She waited next to the ash cans, hopping from one foot to the other, filled with nervous jitters. When the loud bell rang at four o'clock on

the dot, Samantha stood perfectly still. It felt like
forever, but it was really only a minute or two
before Nellie, Jenny, and Bridget appeared. The two
little girls looked so confused and fearful, Samantha
tried to calm them.

"Everything will be all right," she said, though
she was nervous, too. Samantha handed Nellie,
Bridget, and Jenny shawls and scarves to cover up
their orphan uniforms. "So no one will notice us,"
she explained.

With shaking, fumbling hands, Samantha and
Nellie hurriedly helped Bridget and Jenny wrap
themselves up. Just then, *CRASH!* One of the ash
cans fell over. All four girls froze in fear. They heard
a door open.

"Who's out there?" someone shouted.

"Run fast!" hissed Samantha. She and Nellie
herded Bridget and Jenny ahead of them and ran,
their hearts beating hard, as fast as they could run
away from Coldrock House. "Hurry!" Samantha
urged the girls breathlessly. "Hurry!"

They didn't slow down until they were near
Uncle Gard and Aunt Cornelia's house. Jenny
trotted along next to Samantha trustfully. It made

Samantha feel very grown-up—like a big sister—to have Jenny relying on her so completely. She held Jenny's hand very tightly.

Samantha led the way to the alley behind the house. "We'll have to climb in this window to the basement storage room," she explained in a soft voice. "The back stairs start in the basement and go all the way up to the top floor. When we get inside, we'll take our shoes off so that no one will hear us. There's a door that leads to the kitchen right off the stairs, so be very quiet when we pass it. Gertrude may be in the kitchen. She notices everything and she's kind of mean, so just follow me and don't talk. Ready?"

Nellie, Jenny, and Bridget nodded. Samantha climbed through the small window into the dark basement, then reached up to help Jenny through. When they were all inside, Samantha tiptoed to the stairs and started up. There was a lot of noise in the kitchen. Gertrude seemed to be banging pots and pans together, and the laundry wringer was going *thump, thump, thump.*

As quietly as whispers, the four girls climbed the steps up to the main floor, up past the bedroom floor, and up to the very top floor. Samantha put her finger to her lips and slowly, slowly opened the door at the top of the stairs. She peeked her head out and looked around. No one was there. She motioned the three girls to follow her, and they quickly darted into the empty room across the hall.

They all sighed with relief. "Phew!" said Samantha. "I've been holding my breath ever since we climbed in the window. I was about to burst!"

"Me, too!" said Nellie. She looked around the room. Winter sunshine made bright yellow patches of warmth on the thin, faded rug. Samantha had

brought up lots of her books and
toys to make the room look welcoming and homey. Jenny and
Bridget sat right down and started
to play with Samantha's pretty
paper dolls. Nellie smiled when
she saw the blackboard they used to have in the
Mount Better School. "Everything looks very nice,"
she said to Samantha. "Thank you."

"It's a little cold up here," said Samantha. "I'm
sorry you can't have a fire. But I brought up all the
extra blankets I could find. Gertrude's room is right
down the hall. You'll have to be very quiet at night
and early in the morning while she's up here. I hope
you will be all right."

"We'll be fine," Nellie said cheerfully.

Jenny and Bridget were hungry, so Samantha
showed them the box of fruit and bread and cheese
she'd smuggled up to the room. They both took
apples to munch right away. "I couldn't bring very
much," Samantha explained. "Gertrude keeps an
eagle eye on the food in this house. But don't
worry. I'll find a way to bring more next time."

"Nellie," Jenny asked as she played with the

paper dolls, "do we have to go back to Miss Frouchy at the orphanage tonight?"

"No," said Nellie. "We're going to stay here."

Jenny looked glad. "Does that mean we're not orphans anymore?"

"Well . . ." Nellie began.

Samantha knelt down and put her hand on Jenny's shoulder. "You and Bridget and Nellie are still together," she said. "And you'll never be orphans as long as you have one another."

"And good friends like Samantha," added Nellie with a smile.

TOGETHER

For the next few days, Samantha felt as if she lived in two different worlds. In one world, she made valentines and cookies with Aunt Cornelia. She went to school, practiced her ice skating, and joked with Uncle Gard, just as usual. The other world was smaller and quieter, but just as happy. That world was hidden away upstairs, in the room where her secret family lived. Samantha was a very important member of that family. It was up to her to be sure that Nellie, Bridget, and Jenny had food to eat, water for drinking and washing, books to read—everything they needed.

Every morning before dawn, Nellie crept down

the back stairs, climbed out the cellar window, and went about the city looking for work. She was gone all day. Bridget and Jenny stayed in the attic, playing with paper dolls, napping, and whispering quietly together. After their horrible days with their uncle and at the orphanage, they were happy to stay safe and cozy in their secret hideaway. And Nellie was always glad to get back to them at the end of the day.

Samantha loved being with Nellie again, and she liked being a big sister to Bridget and Jenny. Whenever she could manage it, she slipped away to be upstairs with her secret sisters. It was easy for Samantha to keep them happy and amused. They all loved to hear her tell about Aunt Cornelia and Uncle Gard. They asked hundreds of questions. What color dress was Aunt Cornelia wearing today? What did Uncle Gard say when Samantha got an A on a spelling test? Did Aunt Cornelia finish the valentines she was making? What did they look like? When were Aunt Cornelia and Samantha going to give Uncle Gard his valentine? The three girls listened to everything Samantha said with glowing eyes.

"Well," said Jenny one day, "I think your Aunt Cornelia and Uncle Gard are the finest lady and gentleman in New York City!"

"Yes!" agreed Bridget. "The only thing I liked at Coldrock House was when they visited. Once your Uncle Gard gave me a peppermint and Miss Frouchy didn't see," she remembered. "I made that peppermint last a long, long time. I wish I could have another one *right now*."

"I wish you could, too," sighed Samantha.

She was having a hard time finding enough food for the hungry girls. Samantha gave them most of her lunch, all of her afternoon snack, and anything else she could smuggle from the pantry. One day she bought bread at the bakery and hurried home with the loaf hidden under her plaid cape. Another day she tried to bring a pot of cocoa to the girls. Bridget was catching a cold, and Samantha wanted her to have something warm to drink. But Gertrude stopped her at the kitchen door.

"Where are you going with that pot of cocoa?" Gertrude asked sharply.

"Up—upstairs," said Samantha.

"I won't have chocolate spilled all over your bedroom," said Gertrude. "Sit here at the kitchen table and drink it. Though I do not understand why you need to drink a whole pot of cocoa," she scolded. "I've never seen a child eat and drink as much as you have lately. Glass after glass of milk! Tea cakes and sandwiches all the live-long day! All the fruit from the bowl in the dining room! The way food disappears in this house, you'd think we had ten children living here instead of just one."

Samantha gulped her cocoa. Gertrude was getting suspicious!

So the next evening, when Samantha sneaked into the pantry, she tried to be very, very careful. Quietly, she opened the cookie jar. Quietly, she took three of the heart-shaped cookies she and Aunt Cornelia had made. She wanted to have a little party for Nellie, Bridget, and Jenny because the next day was Valentine's Day. She put the cookies in her pocket, turned to go, and there was Gertrude!

Gertrude blocked the doorway, her hands on her hips. "Cookies?" she snapped. "You just had

dinner!" She frowned at Samantha. "Are you
keeping a pet in this house? Is there some animal
up in the attic? Is that what you are feeding?"

"Oh, no!" said Samantha nervously.

"All week I've heard scratches and scurrying
up there at night when I'm in bed," said Gertrude.
"There's *something* up there. I don't know whether
it's mice or thieves or ghosts, but I'll find out sooner
than soon!"

Samantha hurried away with her cookies. *She*
knew what Gertrude was hearing. She'd have to
warn the girls—and fast.

As soon as she was out of Gertrude's sight, she
ran up the stairs. "You're going to have to be quieter
than ever," Samantha panted to Jenny and Bridget.
"Gertrude said she hears noises. And Nellie, maybe
you'd better not go in and out for a few days. I'm
afraid she may catch you on the stairs."

Nellie agreed sadly. "I haven't had any luck
finding work anyway," she said. "No one wants me
for a maid. They think I don't look strong enough."
She sounded discouraged. "I think I'll probably
have to go back to the thread factory where I
worked before we moved to Mount Bedford."

"Don't give up yet, Nellie," said Samantha. "It's only been a few days."

"I know," said Nellie. "But we can't stay here forever."

Samantha knew Nellie was right. But she didn't know what to do.

Then, suddenly, the door flew open and Gertrude stormed in! "Whatever is going on here?" she demanded. "Who are these children? What are they doing here? What have you been up to, Miss Samantha?"

Samantha couldn't think of anything at all to say. She just sat there miserably.

"Well!" said Gertrude with a smirk. "I think you'd better come with me. And these ragamuffins had better come, too. Just wait till your aunt and uncle see this! You certainly have some explaining to do, young lady! Now get downstairs."

Gertrude crossed her arms on her chest and glared at the girls as they filed slowly past her and down the stairs. Samantha's heart sank with every step she took. Her plan had failed. Now the girls would have to go back to Coldrock House. They'd have to face Miss Frouchy and punishment for

"Whatever is going on here?" Gertrude demanded.
"Who are these children? What are they doing here?"

running away. Worse than that, now they would be separated—probably forever. Nellie would be sent away on the orphan train.

Gertrude followed the girls into the parlor where Uncle Gard and Aunt Cornelia were sitting by the fire. When they saw Nellie and her sisters, they both gasped. "Why, Nellie! Bridget, Jenny! What are you doing here?" asked Aunt Cornelia.

"Begging your pardon, madam," said Gertrude, her eyes bright with self-importance. "These raga-muffins were hiding in your attic. Street children! No better than beggars! They've probably been sneaking through your house stealing from you!"

"That's not true!" burst out Samantha. "They'd never take anything!"

"Then who's been stealing all the food?" asked Gertrude.

"I have," said Samantha. She was so mad, she was almost crying. "*I'm* the thief, not them!"

"Now, let's calm down," said Uncle Gard. "Samantha, perhaps you can explain all this."

"Well," she began. But just then Bridget sneezed.

"First, you'd better come sit here and get warm,"

Aunt Cornelia said gently. The four girls sat on the floor in front of the fire.

Samantha began again. "It's my fault. Nellie didn't want to run away from the orphanage. But Miss Frouchy was going to send her away on the orphan train. Bridget and Jenny were too young to go, so they would have had to stay at Coldrock House. They would never have seen Nellie again. So I talked Nellie into coming here, just until she could find a job where they could all be together."

"How long have they been here?" asked Aunt Cornelia.

"About four days," said Samantha.

"Four days!" exclaimed Aunt Cornelia. "But how did they eat?"

"I brought them food," said Samantha. "Gertrude is wrong. They'd never steal."

"I know that's true," said Aunt Cornelia. Uncle Gard didn't say anything. He just stared at the four sad girls.

Aunt Cornelia looked at him. "Well, Gardner," she said. "This is a very serious matter. What do you think we should do with these girls?"

"Give them warm baths and put them to bed,"

said Uncle Gard firmly. "We can decide the rest in the morning."

And that is exactly what they did. That night, Nellie, Bridget, and Jenny slept in Samantha's room. *This is probably the last time we'll be together,* thought Samantha as she watched the girls sleeping. Their faces were pink and peaceful in the firelight.

Late into the night, Samantha heard low murmurs coming from Uncle Gard and Aunt Cornelia's room. She knew they were deciding what to do with Nellie and Bridget and Jenny. Would they send them back to Coldrock House? Would they let them stay for just a little while longer? Would they try to find Nellie's uncle? Finally, Samantha couldn't wonder or worry any longer. She fell asleep.

The next morning when the girls came downstairs, there were three more places set at the breakfast table. And at every place there was a big red heart trimmed with lace.

"Happy Valentine's Day, girls," said Aunt Cornelia.

"Happy Valentine's Day," they all replied.

"Let's have breakfast," Uncle Gard said cheerfully.

The four girls sat down. But before she could swallow a crumb, Samantha's curiosity made her burst out, "Uncle Gard, Aunt Cornelia, have you decided? What are you going to do about Nellie and Bridget and Jenny? Couldn't they please stay here? They wouldn't be any trouble, and they'd be a big help around the house. They've all been taught to be maids . . ."

"We don't need any more maids," said Aunt Cornelia.

Samantha's heart sank.

"But we do need more girls here," said Uncle Gard. "I'd say we need three more girls, in a variety of sizes: tiny, medium, and still not very big." He turned to Nellie. "Miss Nellie O'Malley, how would you and Bridget and Jenny like to stay here? You could be sisters to Samantha and daughters to Cornelia and me."

Nellie looked very serious. "We would like it very, very much," she answered.

"Hurray!" shouted Samantha. She bounced out of her chair and ran to hug Aunt Cornelia, then Nellie, Bridget, and Jenny. Then all four girls hugged Uncle Gard and showered him with kisses.

"Well," smiled Uncle Gard, "what a lovely Valentine's Day this turned out to be! I have *five* of the sweetest valentines anyone could ever have. I must be the luckiest person in the world!"

Samantha laughed. "No, Uncle Gard," she said. "*I'm* the luckiest person in the world. At last, at last, I have a real family of my own!"

LOOKING BACK

CHANGES
FOR AMERICA
IN
1904

American families relaxed on Sunday afternoon drives.

Wherever turn-of-the-century Americans looked, they saw a changing world. Automobiles were taking the place of horses even on country roads. By the time Samantha was nineteen years old, the Ford Motor Company had built over a million cars—all of them black! A new car came off the assembly line every three minutes. Trains linked every corner of the country. They could travel from New York to California in just four days. Today, jet planes make that same trip in six hours, but there were no jets at the turn of the century. The airplane, that "crazy, dangerous, newfangled contraption" the Wright brothers flew in 1903,

The Wright brothers' airplane didn't carry passengers.

New York was already a big city in Samantha's time.

wasn't used for passengers until Samantha was forty years old!

Cities continued to grow bigger and bigger as Samantha grew up. Every day hundreds of young people left their homes on America's farms to look for city jobs. Thousands of immigrants poured into American cities from all over the world. When they first arrived, most immigrants could not speak English. Some people made fun of them and only let them work as servants

or peddlers, or in city factories for long hours at low pay. Many immigrants had to live in crowded, run-down tenements and slums. But the immigrants still found opportunities in this country. They worked hard to learn a new language, get better

In 1907, more immigrants than ever before came to America.

363

These farm girls took city jobs to earn money.

jobs, and earn more money. Soon they enjoyed a good life in their new land and became proud and respected Americans.

As Samantha grew up, more and more Americans obeyed the laws that said all children—rich and poor, boys and girls— should go to school until they were sixteen. Education helped young women get jobs and earn money to take care of themselves.

Back in the days when Grandmary was young, it wasn't proper for young ladies to even talk about money, and they certainly couldn't think about earning it! They were expected to live at home with their families until they got married and had husbands to take care of them. But by the time Samantha was old enough to work, people's attitudes had begun to change. Women could get jobs in department stores or in offices as secretaries—a job that only men had held before! Many women became phone operators, since more and more homes and offices had telephones.

Women who had gone to college became teachers or worked in a new profession called social work. One of the

Women worked as secretaries and telephone operators.

most famous social workers was a woman named Jane Addams, who founded Hull House, a settlement house that helped immigrants in Chicago learn English and trained them for work.

Even though women could finally have jobs and earn their own money, it still wasn't proper for them to live

Jane Addams, who founded Hull House in 1889, worked there her entire life.

alone. So there were special women's hotels and boarding houses where America's "working girls" could live and be carefully *chaperoned*, or looked after.

Once a young woman like Samantha got married, she quit her job, moved to a home of her own, and began to raise a family. Her home, like most in America, would have many "modern" inventions. Even people who were not wealthy had electric lamps, running water, gas stoves,

The Lamp that Lights the Way to Lighter Housework

Electricity made housework easier.

When Samantha grew up, mothers and daughters did housework together.

refrigerators, and washing machines. Samantha would have needed these new machines to make housework easier because it was hard to find people who wanted to be servants. The immigrants who had been Grandmary's and Cornelia's maids had gotten better jobs, so a woman like Samantha had to do many chores herself.

Since there were few servants willing to take care of elaborate clothes like women wore at the turn of the century, fashions began to change, too. New styles were simpler to take care of and easier to wear. Back when Grandmary was a young woman, her long skirts and petticoats with layers of ruffles might have weighed as much as 25 pounds. Young women like Cornelia raised their hemlines a bit and stopped squeezing themselves into tight corsets that made

As a young woman, Grandmary would have worn a dress like this.

it hard to move and even to breathe. By the time Samantha was a young woman, skirts were even shorter and clothing was even looser. These new styles upset some people. There were even some laws that said

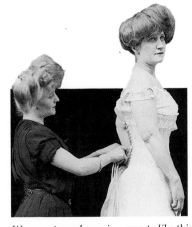

Women stopped wearing corsets like this.

women would have to pay a fine and go to jail if their skirts were more than three inches above the ankle!

But women liked the new freedom that shorter, more comfortable clothing gave them. These new styles seemed to be signs of the way women thought about themselves—as active people who had places to go and work to do. They were women who would not be hemmed in by old-fashioned clothing or old-fashioned attitudes.

904   1909   1914   1919   1924   1929

As times changed, women shortened their dresses.

MEET THE AUTHORS

SUSAN ADLER loved learning about what America was like in 1904 while she wrote about Samantha. Now she continues to learn about other times and places through her work in art conservation. Ms. Adler lives with her family on the East Coast.

VALERIE TRIPP says that she became a writer because of the kind of person she is. She says she's curious, and writing requires you to be interested in everything. Talking is her favorite sport, and writing is a way of talking on paper. She's a daydreamer, which helps her come up with her ideas. And she loves words. She even loves the struggle to come up with just the right words as she writes and rewrites. Ms. Tripp lives in Maryland with her husband and daughter.

MEET THE ILLUSTRATOR

DAN ANDREASEN always wanted to be an artist. As a child, he copied drawings by Leonardo da Vinci from art books that he checked out of the library. Mr. Andreasen lives in Florida with his wife and three children.

Read Nellie's story, too!

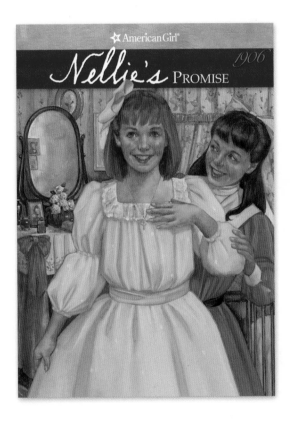

Nellie O'Malley finally has a home again. She and her little sisters, Bridget and Jenny, are happily settling in with Samantha's family in New York City. Uncle Gard and Aunt Cornelia even plan to adopt the girls. Then Uncle Mike shows up and threatens to ruin everything!